This book is a work of fiction.

Any similarity to persons living or dead is purely coincidental.

Cover Photo by MRBIG_Photography/iStockphoto.com
Cover Design by Coverlüv

THORN
A Lords of Carnage MC
Romance

DAPHNE LOVELING

Copyright © 2018 Daphne Loveling
All rights reserved.
ISBN-13:
978-1985133105

ISBN-10:
1985133105

I don't usually make playlists for my books, even though sometimes there are songs in my head that won't go away while I'm writing. Those songs make their way into the feel of the book, one way or another. I imagine my characters listening to them. I imagine that the songs make them feel the way they make me feel when I hear them.

This book's song is "Cover Me Up," by Jason Isbell. If you don't know it, you should. It's a song about transition, and redemption, and how scary it is to open yourself up. I think about Thorn now, every time I hear it.

I hope you find a love as true as Thorn did.

Love, Daphne

DAPHNE LOVELING

1
ISABEL

"Izzy, come *on!*" my best friend Deb cries.

"Jeez, I'm coming!" I retort, trying not to wobble on these insanely high heels I borrowed from her.

The back entrance we're heading toward definitely doesn't look like it's for customers. But the dimly-lit parking lot of the roadhouse was full, so Deb ended up having to park way in back, next to a dumpster. We're not wearing coats against the early November chill, and this door was propped open with a rock, so of course Deb made a beeline for it to get inside as quickly as possible.

I shoot one last glance back into the parking lot, just to check for myself that there's no one watching or following us. Reassured, I slip through the heavy steel door behind my friend.

Buzzy's Roadhouse is a few miles outside the city limits. I've never been here before, but Deb says she came here once with her brother. The building itself is a wreck. The outside is poorly constructed clapboard and faded siding that makes it look like it's likely to fall down in the next strong storm. Inside, it smells like smoke and body odor. The lights are so dim you can barely see anything.

Buzzy's is known for being a dangerous place. Somewhere no "decent" girl would go — especially unaccompanied by a male companion. People turn in curiosity to look at Deb and me as we walk in. We're clearly not regulars, and they probably think we're scared. Or at least, that we *should* be.

But most people don't know my father, or the family I grew up in. This? This is *nothing*.

Deb, on the other hand, probably ought to have thought twice before coming here. Or at least she should be less eager and excited than she is. But as long as I've known her, Deb has never been afraid of anything. She's always been the kind of girl to run toward the fire instead of away from it.

Paradoxically, of the two of us, I'm the more cautious one. Not because I'm afraid, but because my life has had more than enough chaos in it already.

Deb's dad is an important lawyer in our town. She grew up with a silver spoon in her mouth. But hey, we always want what we don't have, right? So of course, Deb has always been tempted by walking on the wild side, the wrong side of the tracks. She loves the idea of coming here to Buzzy's to find some dangerous, shady guys to flirt with.

As for me, I'm usually happy to curl up with a book and spend my evening that way. But these days, since I've basically been under house arrest for the last month, I was more than willing to break out and have a little fun at Deb's request. Besides, as shabby and potentially dangerous as Buzzy's is, it does have two major things going for it.

One: none of the dumbasses we knew from high school are likely to be here.

And two: neither is anyone from my dad's club.

Once we're inside, I finally start to relax. The prospect of a couple of hours of freedom is a happy one. I follow Deb through a dubious-looking hallway. We pass a couple of closed doors with faded, smoke-stained signs labeling them. As we go by the men's bathroom, a door opens, and a large, beer-gutted man comes out. The stench he leaves behind wafts into the hallway. I reflexively wrinkle my nose and take a step back in disgust. But Deb, excited as she is, doesn't even seem to notice.

"Come on!" she calls again, reaching back to grab my hand. She practically drags me toward the bar, and I almost stumble on my high heels trying to keep up with her.

Inside the main room, the din of music and voices is deafening. The smell of sweaty bodies is worse in here. It's just short of stifling. My lungs feel like they need a big, deep gulp of fresh air, but there's none to be had in this crowded room. Instead, I take shallow breaths through my mouth and try to ignore the odors.

Deb makes a beeline for the bar to get us drinks. I watch as she stands up to balance on her tiptoes, and leans over the counter to yell our order to the bartender. Her breasts half-spill provocatively from her low-cut dress; the barman stares openly and gives her a wolfish grin.

While she's busy, I take a moment to look around. The place is packed almost wall to wall with people. Most of the men are large, hairy and tattooed, with muscles running to fat. The women are younger, with a few exceptions. They're tarted up, like me, and dressed like offerings to the male population. Clothing-wise, I'm certainly not out of place, although my sluttiest black dress and Deb's heels are actually a little on the conservative side compared to most women here.

Though I'm certainly not scared, I'm already starting to wonder if coming to Buzzy's was a good idea. I came here for a rare night out with my BFF, and away from the gaze of my overprotective father. But I'm starting to wish we'd chosen someplace a little tamer, with a little less testosterone. Sure, I wouldn't mind a little flirting myself. And maybe I was hoping in the back of my mind that there'd be a hot guy my age to do a little lip-locking with. But right now, as the hungry gazes of the males in this bar start to shift toward me, I'm starting to feel like a piece of packaged meat on display. With a neon sign overhead that says *eat me*.

"Here!" Deb calls into my ear, handing me a plastic cup full of beer. "You can get the next round."

I accept the cup from her. We raise our glasses in a mock toast, and I take a drink. It's cold and soothing against the smoke that's burning my throat. I let out a sigh of pleasure, even though the beer itself isn't that good.

"Have you noticed how many guys are staring at us?" I murmur into Deb's ear.

"I know!" she crows happily, and flips her hair back in a flirty, seductive move. "I told you this place would be cool."

"That's not what I..." I shoot back, but before I can finish my sentence, a tall, stocky man with a long dark beard comes up behind Deb and grabs her around the waist.

"Well, well, well, darlin', haven't seen you here before!" the man bellows. "You look good enough to eat!"

Deb laughs and moves out of his grasp to look at him. "Hey," she simpers, cocking her head at him.

"I'm Ralph," he says.

"Deb," she answers. "And this is my friend Izzy."

"You girls are new around here," he says, looking each of us over slowly and with obvious pleasure. "I'da noticed you around."

"You a regular, then?" I reply. Distaste tinges my voice, but he doesn't seem to notice. He's not bad looking, honestly, although he's not really my type. But he's so obviously looking to score with anything in a skirt that I'm immediately turned off. Deb, however, doesn't seem to share my feelings.

"Here every weekend," he says proudly. I just manage to stop myself from snorting. "Wished I'd seen you before. I coulda bought your drinks for you."

"There's always the next round," Deb smirks, and bats her eyes at him. *Oh, brother.*

Ralph takes this for the invitation it probably is, and takes a step toward Deb. He pulls her close and cops a feel of her ass. "You are *tasty*," he leers.

"How would you know?" Deb shoots back. "You haven't tasted me yet."

Then before I even know what's happening, Ralph's tongue is so far down Deb's throat I'm pretty sure he's checking to see whether she still has tonsils.

If you've ever had to stand around while two people suck face in front of you, you'll have some idea of how awkward this is. I take a long sip of my beer, and look around the room like the clientele is fascinating. But when I look back, Deb and Ralph are *still* going at it. Ralph's got his hand on her thigh and he's inching his hand under her dress. Deb's not doing anything to stop him. In exasperation, I wonder whether they're going to start going at it right here, in full view of everyone.

"Um, guys?" I say snarkily. "Really?"

Deb breaks away from Ralph's mouth and gives me a little pout. "Come on, Izzy. We're just having a little fun."

Ralph looks up at me, and flashes me a wink that he probably thinks is sexy. "Are you ladies a twofer?" he asks with a leer.

Ugh. Gross. "No," I reply crossly, but Deb actually *laughs*.

"What's the matter, handsome? Am I not enough for you?" she whines, placing a hand on his forearm.

"More than enough," he growls. "Let's take this somewhere else. I got a truck out in the parking lot. Back seat of the cab's pretty comfy."

Deb flashes me a half-apologetic glance. "I'll be back in a few, Iz, okay?"

Suppressing a sigh, I wave her off. "Fine. I'll be here."

"The offer still stands," Ralph tells me. I shoot him a disgusted look. "Suit yourself, candy ass."

Ralph leads Deb out the front door, nodding to the bouncer on the way. I take a deep breath and let it out, then look toward the bar for a free stool. Looks like I'm going to be here for a little while.

With a little difficulty, I slide up onto the only unoccupied bar stool I see and try to make myself invisible. I'd much rather be an observer than one of the observed, especially while Deb is off having fun with Ralph. Absent-mindedly, I finger the small gold starfish that I wear on a chain around my neck and glance around the room. It's kind of amusing, actually. The guys in this bar are all puffing and posturing, trying to look tough and dangerous. They don't scare me, though. They look like pansies compared to the guys in my dad's club, the Death Devils. My dad, Oz, is the president of the MC. And as much as I've grown to hate the club and everything associated with it, I have to admit they're ten times the men that these guys are.

Still, I'm definitely attracting attention, and I can tell I'm not going to be alone for much longer. Reflexively I reach in my purse and finger my pepper spray, reassured that it's there in case I need it.

"Hey. You look lonely." A hint of beer breath comes wafting toward my nostrils. Grimacing slightly, I turn to see a greasy-looking guy with unwashed shoulder-length hair staring at me with an expectant grin.

"No. I'm really not," I tell him, and turn away. But of course, he's not about to be deterred so easily.

"Oh, come on, girly. Give me a smile. I bet you're beautiful when you smile."

Ugh. "Sorry, but I don't owe you a smile, or anything else. I just want to sit here and be left alone, thanks."

I should have known my refusal would set the greasy stranger off. "You're kind of a bitch, you know that?" he snarls.

"Yeah. I know," I hurl back. "So leave me the fuck alone."

Asshole leans over in the other direction and mutters something, and then a moment later there's a second man standing in front of me. "What the fuck is your problem, bitch?" he challenges me. "My friend here was just trying to offer you a drink."

"No, he wasn't," I retort. "He was trying to get into my pants. Which are closed for business. So there's no need to keep making conversation."

I turn away towards the bar, but the second guy grabs my bicep and pulls me back around.

"What are you, a fuckin' dyke?" He's towering over me now, flecks of spittle appearing on his lips as his face contorts into an angry mask. I know he thinks he's scaring me, but fuck that shit. I've had enough of this bullshit.

"Yep. I'm a fuckin' dyke," I agree, and stand. "Now, if you'll excuse me. I'm gonna go into the ladies room, and find a hot young girl to eat out, because I *know* I'll do a better job of it than any of the clowns in this bar can."

I stand up and try to shake the second guy's hand off my arm, but he tightens his grip and wrenches me toward him. Bracing myself against the bar for balance, I bring my spiked heel down hard on his foot, crushing it against his boot and breaking off the heel in the process. But it's enough: the guy lets go of my arm and howls in pain.

I make a break for it before the first asshole can grab me, limp-running through the bar toward the hallway where we came in. I don't stop at the bathroom, in case they decide to stand outside the door and wait for me. Instead, I head through the back door out into the parking lot where we came in.

Outside, I keep going until I'm far enough away that I'm not easily seen from the back entrance. In spite of myself, my heart is pounding a little bit as I take a few deep breaths and look around to assess my situation. I'm safe, but my shoe is fucked. And I'm without transportation until Deb is through boinking Ralph in the back of his truck.

The night air is cool, but not so cold that I can't stay out here for a while. I wander over to Deb's car and lean against it. I send her a quick text, which she predictably does not respond to.

For a few minutes, I wait on high alert. No one who looks like the guys who were harassing me comes out the back or the front, so I start to relax a little. I do a scan of the parking lot , looking for a rocking truck, but there are so many pickups here that I'll never be able to see Ralph's in the dark. Since walking is kind of a hassle right now, I settle in to wait for them to finish, figuring I'll catch up with them when they head back toward the bar. Taking out my phone, I decide to pass the time by checking social media for a while.

It's my own stupid fault that I'm not paying as much attention as I should to the comings and goings in the parking lot. My father's trained me better than this, but for some reason his training has momentarily gone out the window. Which is why the soft rustling behind me doesn't register in my conscious brain for a second.

Turns out, it's a second too long.

Before I know what's happening, a rough hand has clamped itself over my mouth. My phone flies from my hands as my arms are wrenched behind my back. I start to scream as a hood is pulled roughly over my head. Before I can try to thrash away, my wrists are bound, and I'm being lifted and carried in the opposite direction from the bar.

I hear a van door open, and I'm tossed roughly into the back. Whoever nabbed me climbs in beside me, making the shocks dip, and the door slides shut. A key turns, the engine starts, and the van pulls away and accelerates quickly, driving off into the night.

2
THORN

"Prospect! Where the fuck is my bike?"

The gangly kid startles and turns to look at me wide-eyed. He's still wet behind the ears — doesn't look any more than eighteen, though I know he's a few years older than that. The newish-looking tattoos that line his stringy arms look like they're serving as some sort of inadequate armor.

"It's outside, sir," he stammers. "I just got done washing it, like you asked."

"No it's fecking not!" I sneer at him. "I didn't give yeh permission to move the thing, yeh gobshite."

"I didn't!" he insists, and swear to God, he raises a shaky hand. "I swear, Thorn, I didn't do anything to it!"

"Then where the feck is it?"

He's still staring at me in terror and disbelief as I shove his shoulder roughly toward the front door and motion for him to go outside. He pushes the door open and holds it for me, then trots ahead of me to the side of the lot where the hoses are.

My bike is nowhere to be seen. I think he's gonna shit his pants right then and there.

"Oh my God!" he yells. "It's gone! I don't know where it is! I swear! I don't know!" His head is shaking back and forth so fast it looks like it's about to fly right off his neck.

"Well, you had the charge of it, didn't yeh?" I growl, taking an angry step toward him. I make a show of pushing up my sleeves and coming at him with clenched fists. "Yeh'd better find it, then, or I'll rip yer feckin' head off yer neck, boyo!"

"Jesus fuck, quit torturing the prospect, Thorn," Beast drawls lazily as he comes up behind me. "And lay off the fuckin' leprechaun act. Jesus, you sound like a fuckin' Irish cop from an old-time movie."

I turn and flash my brother a grin. "All part of the role, brother." I let my accent slide back into its natural slight brogue. I grew up in Ireland, true. But I've lived here in the States for long enough that most of my accent's gone. Unless I've been drinking, that is — in which case my brothers tell me it comes back with a vengeance.

Fucking with prospects is a time-honored tradition. And I'm a man who respects tradition. Besides, Beast is a fine one to talk. He's legend for putting young hopefuls through their paces. I should know: I was a prospect once myself, and Beast accidentally shot me during a prank gone wrong. I'm lucky I lived to tell the tale. But do you catch me holding it against him? You do not.

Since Beast has ruined the fun, I bark out a laugh and nod over toward the other side of the lot. "You'll see my bike's just over there," I say to the prospect's pale, sweating face. "I moved it. To teach you a lesson. As long as one of our bikes is under your supervision, you're responsible for whatever happens to it. Don't you forget that."

We don't refer to prospects by their names — the idea being that they're unimportant and interchangeable to us, until they've proven their worth and get patched in. Or until they've proven their worthlessness and get kicked out. I've heard another prospect call this one Hollis, though I don't know whether that's his given name or his family name. Hollis's head nods up and down like a bobblehead doll. "Yes, sir. I will, sir."

"Good."

"Thorn," Beast grunts. "Rock wants to see you. He sent me out here to find you."

I nod and turn back to the prospect. "I'll check the bike later to see how good a job you did of washing her.

Meantime, take one of the cages to the store and pick up some Guinness. And some Lucky Charms."

The prospect laughs. "Good one."

I look at him sharply. "What?"

His face turns uncertain. "I mean… You know. Lucky Charms. Irish. Leprechaun."

"*I fuckin' like Lucky Charms!*" I roar at him. "Get the fuck out of my face and do what you're told!"

Wide-eyed and white as a sheet, the prospect runs off to do my bidding like his ass is on fire.

"God, you're an asshole," Beast mutters.

I laugh. "At least I haven't shot him yet, fuckface."

With that job done, I go off in search of Rock, our prez. I find him in the chapel with our vice-prez Angel.

"Hey, boss," I call as I walk through the heavy oak door. Rock is sitting at his usual spot at the head of the table. To his right, Angel is reclining in his chair with his feet up, hands laced behind his head. "Angel."

"Brother," Angel nods.

"Have a seat," Rock rumbles.

I do as I'm asked, quickly scanning their faces for any trace of what this is about. They don't look too serious, which is a good sign. But the fact that they're both here, and that we're in the chapel, tells me this is a little more than just a casual conversation.

"What's up?" I ask as I lean back and eye them both.

"I've got a job for you," Rock says without preamble.

"What kind of job?"

"Protection."

The club offers protection to a number of businesses here in Tanner Springs, in exchange for a small fee or some other type of arrangement. I immediately assume this is what Rock's talking about. "Okay," I nod. "Who?"

Rock hesitates. Angel glances at him, and then at me.

"Oz Mandias's daughter," he says.

What. The. Fuck?

"I'm sorry, what?" I ask. "Oz's fuckin' *daughter*?"

"Your hearing is excellent," Rock mutters, narrowing his eyes.

Oz Mandias. The president of the Death Devils. A rival club to our east. We've done business with them before — some drugs, primarily guns. Recently, our two clubs have been approaching something like an alliance. Kind of a mutual back-scratching arrangement. With a vague promise of mutual aid in case of infiltration from other clubs to the south of us.

Mutual aid. Like, providing backup muscle. Extra protection on runs. Things like that.

But *babysitting*?

"I didn't even know Oz had a daughter," I say stupidly. I'm stalling for time, because I don't know what the fuck this is, but everything in my head is screaming *no fucking way I'm doing this*.

"Apparently," Angel says mildly. He leans back further in his chair and shrugs slightly. "I guess she's his only kid. Name's Isabel."

"Jaysus," I mutter, running a rough hand through my hair. "What's the problem? She in danger?"

"Don't know." Rock shifts in his seat and grabs a pack of cigarettes sitting in front of him. Lighting up, he continues. "Oz wouldn't tell me the details."

"Why the hell doesn't he put one of his own men on it?"

I'm envisioning being posted outside the girl's fuckin' high school or something. I can't even imagine how old Oz's daughter would be. The prez of the Death Devils has one of those craggy, weather-worn faces that seems ageless. He could be anywhere from thirty-five to fuckin' sixty, how the hell would I know? The only indication is that his beard has a few flecks of gray in it, but that could just be due to the hard life he's led.

"Well, that's the thing," Rock begins, leaning forward and putting his elbows on the table. "Oz wants her out of sight. And somewhere not connected to their club. That's why he's not putting any of the Devils on it."

Angel laughs again. "Yeah. And probably because he can't trust his men to keep their hands off her."

"Shit, are you kidding me?" Rock tosses back. "Can you imagine what Oz would do if he found out one of his men was screwing his daughter?" He mimes pulling out his dick and cutting it off with a knife.

So. She must be at least past puberty, this girl. *Fuckin' great.* Although I guess I should be relieved that I'm not being asked to protect a little kid.

My blood runs icy in my veins at the thought. A flash of the darkness — the darkness I try never to think of — erupts behind my forehead. It threatens to grow large, but I close my eyes and push it back. Even so, my heart starts to thud erratically in my chest.

I don't want to protect someone helpless. I don't want to do this. I can't…

With an effort that's almost more than I have in me, I take a deep breath and open my eyes again, hoping to Christ I'm quick enough that Angel and Rock won't notice anything. But Angel's peering at me curiously.

"Why are you choosing me for this?" I say quickly, to keep him from asking me whatever question is in his eyes.

"Actually," Rock replies, "Oz is the one who chose you."

"*Oz* chose me?" I didn't even know he'd be able to identify me by name.

"Yeah," Angel snorts. "He said, 'I want the Irish cunt'."

Rock laughs, but I'm still too stunned to join him. "Fuck you, Angel," I growl. "What the fuck does he want me for?"

"Apparently, he's done his research on you," Rock says mildly. "He chose you because he knows you'll do anything to protect her, *and* to keep this away from the cops." A corner of his mouth goes up. "He said he knows he can get your ass deported if you fuck up."

Shit. That's undeniably fucking true. I've got a prison record in the U.S. that's just bad enough one more trip to jail could wind me up on the next plane back to Ireland. And I do not want to go back to Ireland. What's waiting for me there is worse than death.

And then after that, maybe death.

"How the fuck am I supposed to protect this girl, when I don't even know what I'm protecting her from?" I say helplessly, reaching for my own pack of smokes.

"Oz told me to give you this number," Rock says. He pulls a slip of paper out of his jeans pocket and hands it to me. "He'll give you as much information as he wants you to know." He takes a long drag of his cigarette and lets it out. "We're going to set you up in our safe house outside of Connegut River. Not even Oz knows where it is. Oz will have us meet up with some of his men, do the transfer of the girl, then we'll bring her up there. I'll send up a couple of the Lords periodically with supplies, for as long as it takes for whatever shit to die down."

"Wait a minute," I explode. "I'm gonna be holed up at *Connegut* with this girl? Indefinitely?"

"Oz says maybe a couple weeks. Maybe a month. Long enough for them to deal with their problem, till it's safe enough for Isabel to come back."

"Fuck me runnin,'" I mutter.

"Do not fuck this up, Thorn," Rock growls as I stuff the slip of paper into my pocket. "I don't have to remind you how important our alliance with the Death Devils is."

"No. You don't," I agree.

"And keep your dick in your pants."

No worries there. I'd have to be a fucking idiot to screw Oz's daughter. And I'm not a fucking idiot.

And so there it is. I'm doing this thing.

I get up from the table, shoot Rock and Angel each a look, and leave the chapel without a word. I think I catch Angel giving me a sympathetic eye on my way out.

This is happening. I have to obey my president. I have no choice in the matter.

I'm gonna be stuck out in the middle of nowhere playing bodyguard, protecting some snatch from the wolves for the fuckin' duration.

Or die trying.

3
ISABEL

The disgusting rag that's in my mouth smells of motor oil and decay. The rough, dirty feel of it on my tongue makes me want to gag, but I force myself to calm down and breathe through my nose.

The air is stale in the bag that's over my head. I'm fighting a creeping sense of claustrophobia because I can't get a deep breath.

My feet are tightly bound now, along with my hands, with what feel like zip ties. I'm lying on the back bench seat of a van. The seat material is slippery, and I have to keep my knees pressed against the seat in front of me to avoid falling to the floor. Except for the sound of the engine revving and slowing, it's eerily quiet. I realize that none of the men — assuming they're all men — has said a word since they abducted me.

Their silence is what scares me the most. They seem so calm. So deliberate. Whoever they are, they don't seem to care at all about getting anything from me. Not money, information, or even sex. They're treating me like an inanimate object. Like a package to be delivered.

Whatever they want me for, it feels like a done deal. They've already decided what they're doing with me. And I'm helpless to resist. I can't struggle, or beg, or even move. I can't do *anything*.

I may already be dead, and not even know it yet.

My breathing speeds up as my heart begins to race. The thudding is so insistent in my chest that I feel like it's going to burst through my skin. I wonder if it's possible I'm starting to have a heart attack from the fear. Suppressing a moan, I take a long breath in and close my eyes, willing myself to concentrate and slow my respiration. Hold it for a second, then another. Then back out, just as slowly.

In. Out. In. Out.

My heart begins to thud a little less rapidly. I keep breathing, forcing myself to focus just on that. Not to think about anything else. After a minute or so, I start to calm down just a little. My eyes still closed, even though the bag's still over my head, I try to take stock of my situation as best I can. I flex my feet. The zip tie around my ankles is tight, but my circulation's still okay. Both my sandals are still on, the heel on the right one broken off and gone now. I flex my fingers, which are starting to go a little numb.

I shrug my shoulders experimentally, and feel the strap of my small bag pulling against my skin. They never took it off of me when they tied me up. The realization gives me just the slightest source of hope. *Maybe, just maybe, I can keep them from noticing I have my bag long enough to get to my pepper spray…*

A loud thud shakes the frame of the van as we go over a large bump. With nothing to steady me, I fly off the backseat and land painfully on the floor, hitting my head against something sharp. I let out a muffled cry of pain. In front of me, one of the men mutters a curse. I hear a body slide across upholstery, and then rough hands are pulling me up and back onto the seat.

Through the haze of pain, I hear a voice. "She okay?"

"Shut the fuck up!" another one hisses.

It's not much, but it's enough. Enough for me to realize that I recognize the second voice.

It's one of my dad's men. One of the Death Devils. Lazarus, I think.

The realization slices through the throbbing in my head, flooding my body all at once. I feel weak with relief for one dizzying second, almost to the point where I want to laugh. But then confusion starts override the relief, followed by dread. *Am I* sure *that's Lazarus, or only imagining it? I only heard a couple of words, after all. And why would Dad's men fucking* kidnap *me?*

Suddenly, I *need* to know for certain that it was his voice. I need to do something to make them talk more.

Tensing up and ignoring the pounding in the back of my head, I ready my body for the next abrupt motion of the van. Sure enough, about two minutes later, the driver hits the breaks a little abruptly, and I take the opportunity to roll back off the seat and onto the floor.

This time I take the impact on my knee and shoulder, so the sound of me landing is louder than the first time. It hurts like a motherfucker, which is helpful because I don't even have to act: I double over and begin crying out as loudly as the rag in my mouth will allow.

"Goddamnit," someone mutters, and I hear the scrambling again as I'm hauled up. I keep myself doubled up once I'm back on the seat and start to rock back and forth. A rough hand reaches under the hood and pulls the rag out. "What the fuck is wrong with you?" a raspy voice says savagely. I can tell he's trying to disguise his tone, but it's not enough.

"Why didn't you belt me in if you didn't want me to fall off the seat, Franco?" I spit back. The moment of silence that greets me tells me I've hit my mark.

"Shut up," he grits next to my ear.

I could cry, I'm so thankful. But I will myself to calm my voice so it doesn't shake. "What's with all the drama, guys?" I continue in a taunting voice. "You could have just asked nicely, you know."

One of the men snorts. "Just keep quiet and do what you're told," he barks.

"If you're taking me to my dad, why don't you just do it? What's with the bag over my head? It's not like I don't know where the clubhouse is."

"We're not taking you to Oz."

This news is a surprise, and it pulls me up short. The sound of a seatbelt unfurling hums past my ear, and I'm belted in roughly as I struggle to make sense of this.

For one terrible moment, I think…

But no. I know my dad has done unspeakable things to his enemies in the past. He's killed more men, or had them killed, than I ever want to know. Still, he'd never hurt *me*. I can't imagine it. Sure, there's no love lost between us. And I piss my father off on the regular. Most of the time, it seems like he considers me more of an annoyance than anything. But even if he *hated* me, his sense of family is too strong to have me hurt or killed.

He could send you away, though.

As soon as the thought forms in my head I'm absolutely *sure* that's what's happening. A cold pit of dread opens up in my stomach. *No!* I resist the urge to scream, to fight, to argue, because it wouldn't do any good, anyway. If I start yelling, they'll just shove the rag back in my mouth. And besides, there's nothing I could possibly say or do to get them to go against my father's wishes. If I know one thing about the Death Devils MC, it's that not a single one of them would ever disobey a direct order from their president. My father has an iron grip on authority in the club. He could tell any one of them to hold a gun to their heads and shoot themselves, and they'd probably do it without question.

"Where are we going?" I ask uselessly. My voice sounds defeated and small, and I *hate* it.

"None of your business."

"How much longer?" I try again. "I have to pee."

No one even bothers to reply.

We continue to ride in silence, the damn bag still on my head so I can't see shit. I'm starting to feel a little woozy from the lack of air and the motion of the van. I ask once if they can at least lift the bag up a little so I can breathe, but it's like I never even spoke.

Huffing with irritation, I slide my body so that my left shoulder is leaning against the back rest, and try to ease up on the tension from the zip tie cutting into my wrists. *Goddamnit, I'm being treated like a fucking hostage.* When I see Oz, I'm gonna tell him how rough these guys treated me, I tell myself with bravado.

If I see him.

Again, I wonder where the Devils could possibly be taking me. Someplace my dad thinks is safe, I assume. But more importantly, out of the way. Oz has been really on edge lately, and it's only gotten worse in the last weeks. I know the club has been having some sort of problems, though of course I have no idea what they are. All I know is whatever is going on, my father has turned into a freaking tyrant where I'm concerned. Enough so that he saw fit to pull me out of the college I've been attending the next state over. He didn't even tell me he was going to do it until he was knocking on the door of my dorm room with two of his guys to pack up my stuff. Three weeks into the fall term, to be exact. I almost had to take the entire semester off. In the end, I was able to cobble together enough online courses to keep it going, for now.

I have no idea why Oz's solution was to bring me back home, rather than just letting me stay at college. But trying to get information out of him is like squeezing blood from a stone. The men of the club don't tell the women what's going on. Not even old ladies or daughters. They say it's for our own protection. But it's maddening as hell.

So, for the past month, Oz has basically had me under house arrest, and I don't even know why. Every time I've pressed him on it, he just waves me away and says, "Not your place to know. Your place is to obey."

Have I mentioned my dad is a bit of a Neanderthal?

At first, I tried my best to be a good, obedient little girl — even though I'm twenty-one freaking years old. I've stayed at home, done my schoolwork, and waited as patiently as I could for the all-clear from Oz that life could go back to normal again. But instead, he's just gotten more paranoid as time passes. And angrier whenever I try to find out what's going on, or when I'll be allowed to resume a normal life again.

I admit that I've been going a little stir-crazy.

So when Deb proposed going out for a few hours tonight, I figured it would be a harmless way to let off some steam. I knew Oz would be at the clubhouse dealing with some business, and estimated I had at least until midnight before there was any chance he'd be home. So, like a thirteen year-old stealing out into the night through her bedroom window, I took a chance and ignored Dad's strict orders to stay home with the doors locked.

It never occurred to me that Oz might have me followed. And I sure as hell didn't bank on being kidnapped by my own father.

And now I'm about to pay for disobeying him. Just like anyone in Dad's world pays for anything other than total obedience. But unlike the Death Devils and their strict code of club justice, I have no idea what the price is that I'll have to pay.

4
THORN

I don't know what I was expecting when the Devils brought Isabel to the meet-up.

But nothing could have prepared me for the angry spitfire struggling to free herself from the men who pulled her from the van.

"What the fuck is this, a hostage situation?" I snarl in disbelief.

"Oz told us she wouldn't come willingly," one of the men mutters, tightening his grip on her bicep as she tries to writhe away from him. "We decided it was better not to give her the choice."

"By fucking *kidnapping* her?" I retort.

The girl is clearly here against her will. And from the looks of it, she wasn't taken from her home. Aside from the hood that's covering her head, she's got on clubbing clothes. She's wearing a little black dress that looks practically painted onto what is objectively a fucking *perfect* body. She's got on high sandals, but the heel on one of them is broken, causing her to stand at a fucked-up angle when she's not trying to land a kick to one of the Devils' legs.

"Why the fuck is she dressed like that?" I demand.

The larger man speaks up. "We nabbed her at Buzzy's Roadhouse."

Nabbed is right, it seems. And not without a struggle. One of her knees is swollen and purpling. In spite of myself, anger flares deep in my belly. There's no cause for this treatment, for fuck's sake. Even the smallest of the men is almost twice her size. I can't imagine Oz would have wanted them to handle her like this.

Next to me, Beast and Gunner are scowling at the situation unfolding in front of us. They don't look any more impressed than I do. I shoot Beast a look, and he shakes his head in disgust.

Isabel's chest is heaving with exertion, rising and falling rapidly as she continues to struggle against the man holding her arm. It's hard not to stare at her tits, cupped as they are by the tight fabric of her dress. Though I try to keep my focus on the job at hand, I can't help but wonder what they'd feel like in my hands. My cock hardens at the thought.

Down, junior. We have work to do.

"I'm going to make a phone call to Oz," I growl at the men holding Isabel. Nodding to Gunner, I murmur, "Don't let them do anything fucked up. And don't let them leave."

"Got you," he mutters back.

I step away, out of the pool of light created by the street lamp we're standing under. We're in Death Devils territory, in a part of town that no one comes to for any good reason. Even the cops tend to stay away from here. Especially at three in the morning at the deserted end of a dead-end street, with nothing but abandoned warehouses as far as one can see. Tossing back one last scowl of disapproval, I dial the number Rock gave me for Oz's phone. It's late, but too fucking bad. I need some answers before I go any further with this.

If I thought Oz might be asleep at this hour, I was wrong. He answers at the end of the first ring. "Yes."

"It's Thorn."

"You at the pickup?"

"Yes I fucking am! What in the hell is going on, Oz?"

"I'm sure I don't know what you mean," he says mildly.

"Your girl here has been brought to me tied up, with a feckin' hood over her head."

If he's surprised, he doesn't let on. "And?"

"I thought I was to be protecting her, Oz. Not kidnapping her, for Christ's sake."

"My daughter doesn't always act in ways that are in her best interests." I hear him pull in a sharp drag from a cigarette, then blow it out. "She was told not to leave the house. She disobeyed me."

"Oz, in our last conversation, all you told me was that you had a credible threat to your girl's safety." I hear my tone harden. "I could use a little more info here. Especially now that I know I'm to be holding her against her will."

There's silence on the other end of the line for a second. I hear him take another drag of his smoke.

"I have many enemies, Thorn," he finally says. "Perhaps no more than any other MC president, but certainly no less."

"Go on."

"One of my enemies is a man named Fowler. Let's just say we had a business deal together that went bad. We disagree as to the reasons." He hesitates. "Fowler is a man who enjoys torture. Not only the physical aspects, but the psychological. And, it seems, this extends to his sexual proclivities. He has been known to abduct the spouses and daughters of his enemies. *Use* them." Oz's voice turns quiet. Deadly. "Take photographic evidence of the process, and send the mementos to them, before killing the women and returning their mutilated bodies."

"Jaysus," I hiss, running a hand through my hair.

"Yes." Oz lets out a deep breath. "So you see, I need Isabel protected and in a safe space until my club can neutralize Fowler and his men."

"Take him out," I specify.

"Correct."

"Does Isabel know this?"

"She knows only that I believe she's in danger," Oz replies. "She was reluctant but obedient at first to stay at home and out of sight. But it's been over a month now, and she's gotten… restless. Defiant." Puff. "Hence, the little stunt she pulled tonight, going out with her friend."

I frown. "Why haven't you told her? Wouldn't she be more willing to stay put if she knew the severity of the threat?"

I can hear the chill in Oz's voice through the phone. "That I told her to do it should be enough."

A-ha. Oz is used to being obeyed. By everyone, it would seem.

"Isabel is my only daughter, Thorn. My only living relative. I cannot protect her and look for this man at the same time. I need to know she is safe. You, my friend, will keep her safe. Your *club* will keep her safe."

There's an implied *or else* at the end of Oz's sentence. I know my club's relationship with the Death Devils will live or die on what happens here. On whether I keep Isabel alive and out of harm's way.

"Understood," I answer, because I have no choice.

The phone clicks. Oz is gone.

"Fuck me," I mutter, shoving it into my jeans. This job, which I never wanted to begin with, just got worse. Not only am I forced to spend the foreseeable future sitting around at Connegut with my thumb up my arse, the girl I'm guarding doesn't even know enough to be grateful for it. And now, the added problem that she does *not* want to be protected. Which means I have to keep her from escaping to boot.

Not to mention the fact that she's both older and hotter than I expected. Even without seeing her face.

What a load of fucking bollocks this is turning out to be.

I run through every curse word I can think of on the way back to Beast and Gunner and the Devils. "Well," I sneer. "It appears we're all sorted. You numb nuts think to bring the girl a change of clothes, at least?"

The one looks at the other, who shakes his head and has the decency to look at least a little abashed.

"Good Christ." I spit on the ground in disgust. "Gunner, will you get Alix to pack a bag for the girl when you get back to Tanner Springs? Bring it to the safe house your next trip up."

Gunner gives me a brief nod at the mention of his old lady. "Will do."

"All right," I say tiredly. "Go on then, your work is done, you fuckin' robots," I snap at Oz's men. "Give her here. Tell your prez to ring me for an update tomorrow."

The smaller of the two men lets go of Isabel's arm, and the larger one thrusts her toward us, looking obviously glad to be rid of his charge. She stumbles a little but rights herself. I take hold of her arm to guide her the last couple of steps. When she's standing in front of me, I reach down and lift her small purse up and over her body, taking it from her. I look inside briefly. Lipstick. Keys with a small canister of pepper spray. Billfold. Nothing surprising.

"Oh. Here." The larger one reaches into his pocket and hands me a mobile phone. "Hers," he says, nodding toward Isabel. I take it, check to make sure it's off, and slip it into her bag.

The Devils climb back into their van. The engine starts, and I barely bother to watch as they drive away. "All right, brothers. Let's get this over with." I take Isabel by the arm again. "I'm sorry, darlin', but you'll have to keep the hood on for the time being. Can't have you seein' where we're going, now can we?"

At first, the girl pulls away from me. "You plannin' on feelin' your way there with your toes?" I ask, amused. I try again, and this time she grudgingly lets me do it. I take a couple of steps, but forget that she's got a broken heel to one of her shoes. She stumbles again, and I pull her up by the biceps. The weight of her pulls at the zip ties that bind her wrists. The girl gives a muffled cry of pain. I look down and see that the ties have cut into her flesh, breaking the skin.

"For fuck's sake," I mutter under my breath. I give her time to get her legs back under her, and once she's righted herself I pull out a knife from my back pocket. I slip it quickly under the tie, severing it. "I've let you loose for now, but don't make me tie you back up again, you understand?"

Her only response is a muffled grunt. For a second, I don't register why, and then it dawns on me.

"Jaysus, you can't be serious?" I shake my head in disbelief as I reach under the hood and pull the rag from her mouth. Just as soon as I've done it, the girl lunges and tries to kick me, aiming wildly with the foot that has the shoe with the broken heel.

"Now then, is that any way to say thank you?" I ask in a hurt tone.

"Fuck you," she hisses.

"That's better," I chuckle.

We continue toward our own van, which is parked a few steps away, the doors open. I help the girl inside, then wait until she slides as far away from me as she can, into the opposite corner. Beast climbs in and takes the seat ahead of her, sprawling out so he's sitting sideways. I get in beside the girl and slam the door. Gunner gets into the driver's seat.

"You thirsty?" I ask her, aware the rag in her mouth might have parched her.

The girl freezes for a moment. Then the hood gives a quick nod.

"Gun. Toss me that water bottle, will you?" I call. He does as I ask. I unscrew the lid. The girl is rubbing at her wrists, and I reach over and grab one of her hands. She startles at the contact for a second. Then, feeling the bottle on her skin, she wraps her fingers around it. Sliding the neck under the hood, she tips her head back and takes a long gulp, then another. Within seconds, the bottle is drained.

I can't help but watch the smooth, creamy skin of her neck as her throat works. The gentle rise of her breasts catch my attention again. I'm not often this close to girls I'm not planning to fuck or currently in the process of fucking. Jaysus, this girl's body is *ripe* for the taking. I'm just starting to realize how hard having her in the same room with me for days, if not weeks, is going to be.

Isabel finishes the water, and with a small sigh, she hands it back to me. "Thank you," she whispers, so softly I almost don't hear it.

"You're welcome," I say evenly, and suppress a smirk. "Hungry?"

The hood nods.

"Beast, grab the girl something she can eat with that hood on," I say, nodding toward the large box of supplies just in front of him. He rummages around, and eventually produces an apple. I take it from him and catch hold of her hand again. It trembles a little, but she doesn't pull away.

"Here. The best I can do for now."

For the next few minutes, the only sounds are the van's engine and the girl's munching. When she's finished, she holds the core quietly until I take it from her. *She's trying to get me to let my guard down with her.* Docile as a lamb for now, it seems.

I don't expect that'll last.

5
ISABEL

Somehow, I end up dozing off in the Devils' van, despite the awkward position I'm in. I'm awakened by the sound of the car door sliding open. Someone cuts the tie binding my ankles. I'm unbuckled, and then pulled out of the seat and hoisted over someone's shoulder like a damn sack of potatoes.

"We're at the dropoff," Lazarus grunts. He carries me a few feet, then dumps me unceremoniously on the ground. I stagger a bit, the foot with the broken heel slipping a little. He pulls me forward, and I fight him a little, but of course it's useless. From listening to the sounds around me, I know there are at least three Devils here, counting whoever is driving the van. I can't talk, or fight, and I can barely walk.

I'm stood up, Lazarus' hand clenching my upper arm. I continue to struggle, just because I can, and almost manage to connect my foot with his ankle. He shakes me roughly enough to rattle my teeth, and I stop.

Footsteps approach in the gravel. More than one set.

"What the fuck is this, a hostage situation?" a male voice growls.

"Oz told us she wouldn't come willingly," Lazarus replies. "We decided it was better not to give her the choice."

"By fucking *kidnapping* her?" the voice asks, sounding angry. Whoever it is has the hint of an accent — Irish, I think? Or Scottish? I'm not sure.

The men continue to argue back and forth. I'm taking it all in, trying to figure out who I'm being given to. My stomach is starting to churn with fright again, but I work to force the fear down.

"I'm going to make a phone call to Oz," the accented voice snarls. I hear him step away from us. There's no banter or conversation among the others as they wait. I strain to hear the conversation between the man and my father, but he's too far away. All I can make out is the frustrated, clipped tone of his voice.

When the man comes back, I'm handed over to him by the Devils. I struggle again, but lose my balance and almost fall. The zip ties cut painfully into my wrists, and I cry out in spite of myself. When I'm standing upright again, the man swears under his breath. Then, suddenly, the zip tie is off.

"I've let you loose for now, but don't make me tie you back up again, you understand?" he murmurs, his voice low and close to my ear. In spite of myself, I shiver a little.

I try to mouth a response around the rag. For a second, he doesn't say anything. When he does, his tone is tinged with disgust and disbelief. "Jaysus, you can't be serious?"

Before I realize what's happening, his hand is reaching under the hood, pulling the rag from my mouth. I take the first deep breath I've had in hours, and then realize my brief opening. Quickly calculating, I pull back with one foot and thrust forward, try to kick him hard in the shin. Unfortunately, I'm too wobbly and off-balance to connect.

Instead of being angry, though, he seems more amused. "Now then, is that any way to say thank you?" he teases me. This infuriates me.

"Fuck you," I spit.

"That's better." The asshole actually *laughs* at me. I'm too pissed to respond.

A few minutes later, we're in another vehicle, and I'm belted in securely, with the hood still over my head. I'm in completely uncharted territory. The only thing I know is that these men aren't the Devils, and that Oz has given me to them. I'm so angry at him, at them, and particularly at the man with the accent that I want to scream, to lash out, to scratch and punch and maybe even kill. But I know I'm in too helpless a position to do much of anything right now. I sit and fume, planning ten different scenarios in my head, all of which involve inflicting great, lingering pain on every single one of these men, including my father.

About half an hour into the drive, I decide to test how much attention these men are paying to me. Slowly, as slowly as I can bear it, I start to inch the hand closest to the window up toward my neck.

"Don't even think about it."

"What?" I snap back. "I have an itch."

"So practice mind over matter."

Cocky bastard. I huff in frustration and sit back, trying to get into a comfortable position. My feet are aching from the heels, and still a little swollen from the zip ties, and I take turns flexing them one by one.

"Why the hell do you still have these things on?"

"I don't know if you've noticed," I spit, "But until recently I wasn't exactly in a position to take them off."

"Well, you are now."

"I don't have any other shoes," I point out.

"Yeah, I noticed there aren't any trainers in your shoulder bag," he says wryly.

At first I resist, but then realize the only person I'm hurting is myself. Grudgingly, I tip forward, reaching down to slip the straps of the sandals over my heels. The relief is instantaneous. I can't suppress a sigh as I take a moment to massage first one foot, then the other.

"Feel better?"

Goddamnit. I *hate* having my every move watched like this. Especially when I can't see a damn thing.

"Are you seriously going to make me wear this hood forever?"

"Not forever. Just until we get where we're going."

"And then what?"

"Then there won't be anything for you to see."

My stomach flops unpleasantly. Mind racing, I picture myself locked up in a basement somewhere, with no windows and no way to get out. I'm already feeling a little car sick, and the fear makes it worse. I start to take deep breaths again, willing myself not to throw up.

"You all right?"

"I'm fine." I won't give him the satisfaction of knowing this is getting to me.

"Good, good," he says, clearly amused. "Settle back and enjoy your flight, then."

Fuck you! my mind screams at him. Huffily, I turn away from his voice, making a point to give him my back to make my message clear. But as I do, I feel a slight tug around my neck, and then the whisper of something sliding down my chest and under my dress.

"Oh, no!" I gasp. Quickly, I reach up, fast enough that the man barks at me.

"No sudden moves!"

Instantly, I freeze, then continue more slowly. I start to reach a hand inside my cleavage, but suddenly I'm grabbed roughly around my wrist. I gasp as his fingers lock around my tender flesh.

"What the hell are you playing at?" he growls suspiciously.

"Nothing!" I stammer. "I swear! I've just… my necklace! I think the clasp broke. It slipped down inside my bra." My cheeks begin to flame.

"You sure you're not hiding a knife of something in there, looking for your chance to pull it out?" he replies, his voice hard and knowing. "It won't go well for you to cross me, girl."

"I was wearing a necklace!" I try again desperately. "Didn't you notice it? Can't you see it's gone?" My voice breaks. "Please! It means a lot to me! I can't lose it!" Under the hood, my eyes fill with tears, and I'm almost grateful my face is covered so he can't see me start to cry. "Please, just let me get it!"

"Sorry, can't take that chance." I hear his body shift.

"But…"

"Keep your hands where they are."

I open my mouth to try again, but as I do, the touch of a hand on my neck makes me jump and freeze in confusion. Warm, strong fingers slide against my skin, moving aside the fabric of my dress. I want to protest — to pull away — but the man's touch, rough and soft at the same time, makes me shiver. Moving lower, he pauses. My breath catches in my throat as he cups my breast, grazing my nipple.

I stifle a moan.

I don't know if the fear I've been feeling for the last couple of hours is making my nerve endings more sensitive, but the touch of this stranger's hand sends a jolt of pleasure through me that takes me completely by surprise. Somehow, suddenly, I'm instantly wet. Shamefully turned on.

The buzzing in my ears is nearly deafening as the man slowly withdraws his hand. The whisper of warm metal against my skin is like an echo of his presence.

"Here," he mutters. He takes my hand and drops the necklace into my palm.

I hold onto it tightly for the rest of the ride. The little arms of the starfish prick my skin, just painful enough to be reassuring. Just painful enough to let me focus on the sensation of it — and to try to forget about what just happened when my captor touched me.

6
THORN

The safe house is on the banks of the Connegut River. It's the only structure around for miles. There's no mailbox at the end of the drive leading up from the gravel road. In fact, there's not much of a driveway at all. Most people would pass right by it and never even notice it was there. Which is by design.

The house itself is more of a cottage. It's rustic, small and simple, with dark wood siding and a small porch out front overlooking the river. The sort of thing I remember seeing in American films when I was a little tyke. It would be a good fishing cabin, I suppose. If I fuckin' fished.

I don't know how long the Lords have owned this place. Hell, I don't even know if we *do* own it. All I know is that members of the club have been coming up here for years. To get away from things, or to hide out for a while. The place has just enough room to be cramped as shit if there's more than a couple people here, but it's a perfect spot if you want to disappear for a while and not be found.

It's also fucking boring as shit out here.

It's still pitch black out when we arrive at Connegut. The clock on my mobile says it's just after three-thirty in the morning. Sun will be up in a few hours. I let out a sigh of disgust as Gunner comes to the end of the weed-ridden drive and pulls up next to the house. I don't know what the fuck I've done to deserve this sort of punishment.

"Here we are, safe and sound," Gunner announces. He looks back at me with a grin and I flip him off.

Beast yanks open the side door and gets out. Without waiting for Isabel to comply, I reach for her arm and slide her toward me. Predictably, she resists.

"What the fuck are you doin'?" I ask irritably. "There's nowhere to go. You don't have a choice."

"I always have a choice," she hisses, her voice muffled by the bag.

I sigh again and shake my head, then reach over and lift her physically out of the van. She starts to struggle, but I pretend to drop her and she yelps and reflexively throws her arms around my neck. Chuckling, I fling her over my shoulder and carry her the rest of the way into the house. She makes little outraged noises the whole way there, like a pissed off kitten.

The house hasn't been used in a while, and the musty smell of it assails my nostrils the second I'm inside. I reach over to flip on the light switch next to the front door. A lone, anemic bulb gives off just enough illumination to see the state of the place. It's dusty, and sparse, and pretty much the way I remember it from the last time I was here.

Behind me, Beast walks in, carrying a large box of supplies. "Gun's bringing your stuff in," he tells me.

"Thanks." I toss Isabel's body a little roughly onto the couch. She immediately scooches herself to the furthest end of it and draws her knees up defensively toward her chest.

Beast nods toward the girl. "You gonna be good here?"

"Yeh." There's no way Isabel is going to get very far out here, even if she tries to escape. She has no shoes to speak of, and at the moment her only clothing is a tight mini-dress that barely covers her tits or her ass. She has no fucking idea where she is. Even if she managed to get loose, in this cold early November weather she'd get hypothermia from exposure, eaten by a wolf, or abducted by some horny, crazy prepper living out here in a shed before she ever managed to find her way back to civilization. I just have to convince her it's not worth the effort. In the meantime, I'll keep her tied up whenever I can't keep an eye on her, until she figures out what's what.

Gunner comes in a few seconds later carrying my duffel and a couple of paper bags. "Toss them over in that corner," I tell him. Beast is throwing perishables into the fridge, which he's just plugged in. I'm glad for the help getting us sorted, though soon I'll have nothing to do but stare at my feet, so I tell them to leave it. "I'll get the rest later."

"Want some help with her?" Beast asks.

"Yeh, I suppose so." I walk over to the couch and reach down to remove the hood, which we don't need anymore. I grasp the fabric and lift.

The sight of her almost knocks me off my feet.

Sitting in front of me is possibly the most beautiful girl I've ever seen. She squints and turns her face away briefly, unaccustomed to even this weak light. But when she turns back to look at me, her flashing dark eyes with their arched brows bore into mine, her expression both a challenge and a promise. Thick, luscious dark hair tumbles past her shoulders in disarray, framing the gorgeous olive skin of her face. A light sprinkling of freckles dots an even, pert little nose. Her lips… oh, *Jesus*, her lips. They're full and bee-stung, free of lipstick, a little parched, and just begging to be kissed. My mouth fairly waters just to look at them.

My eyes travel back down to the swell of her breasts — the breasts I felt through the fabric of her bra only an hour ago. My cock jumps to attention, and in an instant I'm so hard it's almost painful. Clearing my throat, I look back up at her face, which is flushing a pretty shade of pink. She's thinking of it, too, I can tell.

This is the girl I'll be spending every minute of every day with for days and weeks on end. With no other charge than to keep her safe… and to stay the hell away from her.

Jesus *Christ*, I need a smoke. Or a drink. Or a bottle.

"What?" she shoots at me, tossing her head defiantly.

"Nothing," I mutter. I glance toward a straight-back chair sitting next to the couch and turn to Beast. "Let's put her there for now."

"What?" she challenges. "You too scared to leave me loose? Afraid I'll overpower you and get away?"

"No," I snarl, getting right up in her face until she flinches. "I'm worried you're too stupid to realize that if you try to escape, you'll die out there before you ever manage to find another human being."

Anger is the only way I'm going to manage this. Which is fine, because suddenly I'm fucking furious. "Beast!" I order. "Put her in the chair. I'm going out to the van for some rope."

I stomp outside, taking a few deep breaths to calm myself once I'm out on the porch. Gunner's just bringing the last of the supplies in and passes me on the stairs.

"You gonna be good out here?" he asks.

"Why the *Christ* is everyone asking me that?" I explode, resisting the urge to punch something.

"Because you look like someone just killed your pet hamster," Gun laughs.

"Fuck you," I glower. I storm over to the van and grab the long coil of nylon rope. I head back inside, where Isabel is now sitting, barefoot and bare-legged, on the straight-back chair. She flashes me a look of pure loathing, which actually makes me smile tightly. Even though the fact that her head is at my waist level makes me want to fist my hand in her hair and fuck that pretty mouth of hers.

Beast goes outside to bum a fag off Gunner, leaving me alone with the girl.

"Give me your wrist," I say.

The girl puts her hands in her lap and looks up at me, narrowing her eyes.

I reach down without a word and grab one of her hands. She tries to pull away, and I yank her roughly enough that I know it hurts her a little.

"Ouch," she complains.

"Shut up and do as you're told." I tie the rope tightly around her wrist.

"Or what?" Isabel juts out her chin. "My father…"

"Your father isn't my prez. And he isn't here."

"Why are you…"

"None of your damn business," I cut her off. "I don't care what happens to you. I don't care if you're comfortable or happy. I'm here to do my job. And my job is to make sure you don't get killed. That's all."

"Who would be trying to kill me?" she tosses back, eyes flashing.

"None of your business."

"It's none of my business why I'm being held against my will?"

"No."

"God, you're infuriating."

"Good. Maybe you'll get tired of trying to talk to me, then."

I reach down without bothering to ask and grab her other wrist. The necklace she's still holding falls to the floor. Reflexively, she bends down, but I pull her back up.

"Stay still," I bark. I realize I'm about to tie her hands in front of her, and that there'll be nothing to tie her to that way. Fuck, I can't think straight around this girl. Cursing under my breath, I go behind the chair and kneel. I bind her wrists behind her, tightly enough that she can't get out of them, but not so tight as to hurt her. When that's done, I come back to the front and take hold of her ankle. Her foot is ice cold.

"Goddamnit," I seethe, "why didn't you tell me you were cold?"

She actually *laughs*. "I didn't know you cared."

Fucking Christ. I cross the room to my duffel and dig out a clean pair of my socks. Pulling them on her one by one, I tie her ankles securely to the chair legs. When I'm done, I stand up, not looking at her, and go out to the porch.

"All right. She's set."

"You gonna…" Beast starts to ask.

"Get out of here," I interrupt him angrily. "And Gunner, for Christ's sake, bring her back some clothes as soon as you can."

"Will do."

I stand and watch them leave, until the red from their taillights disappears into the dark. Shaking my head at my fate, I turn and go back inside.

Isabel is there, tied up all in a bow like a fuckin' present. Looking at me with those eyes of hers.

"What now?" she smirks. I have to admire her pluck.

"Now, I'm gonna get some shuteye," I tell her, going over and flicking off the light switch. The room is plunged into darkness. "I haven't had any sleep tonight, thanks to you."

"What am *I* supposed to do?" I can only see her silhouette, but her voice is outraged.

"None of my concern," I shrug. Lying down on the couch, I stretch out to my full length and close my eyes. Suddenly I'm fuckin' exhausted. "Just do your best not to try to escape. I'll see you in a few hours."

7
ISABEL

Within minutes, the man's asleep, snoring softly. As though I wasn't even here.

For some reason, the most infuriating part of all of this is being left here in the dark. Like I'm some sort of inanimate object. I sit, seething, imagining all sorts of revenge that I will exact on him once I somehow get myself free. Experimentally, I wriggle my hands and feet, looking for any looseness in the ropes, but it's no use. Clearly he knows how to tie a knot that won't fail.

Minutes pass. Then more minutes. I don't know how long I wait, listening to his snores and the sound of my own breathing. My butt falls asleep, and I shift uncomfortably and try to wake it back up.

As mad as I am, without an audience for my anger, it kind of starts to dissipate after a while. This is the first time since I was abducted by Dad's men that I haven't been mostly occupied by fighting back fear and dread. I take a deep breath and look around at my surroundings. They're mostly obscured by the dark, illuminated only by the small amount of moonlight coming in through the windows. I squint over at the small kitchen, and then look around at the living room with its threadworn furniture. It would almost be quaint and cozy here, with the right company. And if I wasn't being held against my will.

My eyes drift back to the man asleep on the couch. Even in sleep, his body still seems vigilant, somehow. Aware. As though he'd be up and ready to fight in a split second at the slightest sound. In the pale moonlight, I contemplate his features. The dark, heavy brows. The long, straight nose. The shadow of a beard framing sensuous lips. He's extremely handsome, in a rough, unpolished way.

When he's awake, the man's eyes are dark, brooding. Haunted, almost. He is clearly angry that he has to watch over me. He doesn't want to be here.

That makes two of us.

I know nothing about the man except what the rockers tell me on his cut. Like the other two men who brought me here, he's wearing the colors of the Lords of Carnage MC. I don't know anything about them, except that they're a rival club to the Death Devils. I sure as hell didn't know my dad was friendly with them. I wish I knew why he chose them instead of his own club to guard me.

Probably just to get me out of Oz's hair, I think bitterly. Out of sight, out of mind. He's never been interested in being a father. He's never really cared that much at all about my life. I imagine if I'd been a boy, maybe he'd have taken more of an interest. He could have brought a boy up to be part of the MC. He could have groomed him to be president of the club someday. But a girl? She's just an inconvenience. Just someone to lock away and keep safe, so her priceless honor and purity will stay intact.

Snorting in disgust, I shiver and flex my muscles to increase the blood flow. As much as I'm able, I bring my arms closer to my body. It's cold in here. I heard the heat kick on a little while ago, though, so I'm hoping it'll warm up eventually. Glancing at the empty fireplace, I can't help longing for a fire to cozy up to.

I wiggle my toes, and think about the socks on my feet. About the feel of the man's hands on my skin as he pulled them on.

His rough hand on my breast as he searched for my necklace…

I shiver again, but this time it has nothing to do with the cold.

Somehow, I eventually manage to fall asleep in the chair. When I wake up, it's light. There's a mighty crick in my neck, so painful when I try to move it that I wince.

It's warmed up in the cabin a little. And it smells good. Like bacon. Coffee.

Breakfast.

I blink my eyes open. The man is in the kitchen. He's standing over the stove, in the same jeans as before, and a tight black T-shirt that reveals muscled biceps lined with tattoos.

Somehow he must feel my eyes on him, because he cuts his eyes over to look at me. Saying nothing, he merely nods and continues what he's doing. My stomach growls loudly. I haven't had anything except the apple to eat in over twelve hours.

Eventually, he opens a cupboard and takes out a couple of plates. He holds up a pan of what turn out to be eggs and divides them, then pulls the bacon out of another pan and puts the strips on a smaller plate. He carries them out to the table, sets them down, and looks at me.

"Do you drink coffee?" he asks without preamble. I nod my head. He goes back into the kitchen and pours two cups. He doesn't ask if I take anything in mine.

When the coffee's on the table, he comes over to me. I expect him to untie me, but instead he simply picks me up, chair and all, and carries me over to the table. He sets the chair down, roughly enough that my teeth rattle a little.

I snort in disbelief. "What, so you're going to feed me?" I ask sarcastically.

"No." He reaches behind me and unties my hands. When they're free, he goes to his chair, sits down, and begins to eat without another word.

I snort again and roll my eyes, even though he's not even looking at me. But I'm too hungry to protest or wait any longer. Instead, I grab the fork lying beside my plate and dig in.

I've eaten three pieces of bacon and most of my eggs before I know it. When I finally look up from my food, I see him staring at me, one side of his mouth twitching up just a little.

"Hungry, were you?"

I pick up the mug of coffee, savoring the warmth of it in my hands. I take a sip. It's strong, and I grimace a little.

"You don't like your coffee black?"

"I usually take it with milk," I admit.

"There isn't any," he tells me. Then, grudgingly: "I can ask Gunner to bring some when he comes with some clothes for you."

"Thanks." I take another sip. This time I'm ready for the bitter taste. "So. Am I ever going to know your name?"

He shrugs. "There's no reason you shouldn't. Thorn."

It feels like a little victory that he told me without a fight.

"Why the hell are you doing this, Thorn? You're not in my dad's club."

"Because it's my job," he grunts.

"Why is it your job?"

"Because my president told me this is my job."

"Why does your president care?"

"None of your business."

"Dammit, this *is* my business. I'm the one who's being held captive here!"

"Take it up with your father." He picks up a piece of bacon, his face stormy. He's clearly not going to tell me any more.

The rest of breakfast passes in silence. When I finish my coffee, I want to ask him for another cup. But I don't want to give him the satisfaction of me talking first, so I don't. Instead, I take turns pouting and glowering at him. He doesn't even look at me.

When breakfast is over, Thorn collects the plates and silverware and takes them over to the sink. He dumps them in and turns on the faucet, reaching for a sponge on the counter. The sound of the water, plus the coffee I drank, wakes up my bladder. I try to ignore it, in vain. Sighing in frustration, I admit defeat and realize I'm going to have to talk first.

"I have to pee," I announce.

Thorn turns off the water and comes over. Kneeling, he unties my feet and points down a short hallway. "In there."

I don't wait. Standing up, I try to ignore the pain in my legs as the blood rushes back into them. Hobbling a little, I pad into the hallway and find a smallish bathroom with a sink, a toilet, and a tiny shower stall. I reach up to close the door, but a large, strong hand stops it.

"Are you serious?" I ask incredulously.

"No locking the door." His deep brown eyes bore into me. "If you try to open the window, I'll hear you. If you do anything stupid, I'll have Gunner bring a bedpan and you'll do your business out in the living room where I can watch you."

I blanch. The expression on his face tells me he's dead serious. Nodding, I wait as he takes his hand off the door and allows me to shut it. My hand lingers on the knob as I contemplate locking it anyway, but I decide there's no point. This door is flimsy and hollow. If he wanted to break it down, he could do it with a single blow of his fist.

Inside, I pull down my panties and squat, sighing in relief as my bladder empties. As I pee, I look at the window. It's small, but I could definitely fit through it. Maybe I can wait until Thorn lets down his defenses, and then…

"Hurry up in there!"

"Hold your horses!" I yell back crossly. "*Asshole*," I mutter to myself. I finish peeing and wipe, then wash my hands and dry them on a worn, coarse towel hanging from a rack by the sink. I open the door and Thorn is standing right there, leaning against the jamb.

"Seriously, do you get off listening to women pee?" I ask sarcastically.

His eyes glint, their expression going from irritated to wolfish in a heartbeat.

"Do you want to get me off?" he asks, his lips twisting into a lazy, sexy smirk. "Because I can tell you how, Isabel."

I know he's just saying this to shock me into silence. But it works. Suddenly, I'm acutely aware that I'm alone in the woods with a *man* — a sexy, hard, dominant man — and I have basically no defenses against him. He could do whatever he wanted to me. *If* he wanted to. My pulse starts to race — partly from fear, but partly from something else entirely. Because the thought of Thorn doing *things* to me… *dirty* things… excites me more than I care to admit to myself.

"I don't think my *father* would like that," I croak.

"Your father might not. But you would, wouldn't you, little girl?"

My mouth opens and then closes again. My face starts to burn. I slip past him, but his arm shoots out and grabs me by the bicep, pulling me back toward him.

"Wouldn't you?" he repeats, his mouth so close to my ear I can feel the warmth of his breath.

"You're a pig," I whisper.

He laughs and lets me go.

8
THORN

Isabel asks to take a shower. I can't think of any reason not to let her, so I say yes, though I make her keep the bathroom door open. I show her the tiny linen closet to the left of the bathroom, and she picks out a towel to use. Right before she goes in, she looks at me hesitantly, like she wants to ask me a question.

"What is it?" I demand.

"I don't have anything else to wear," she says in a small voice. "Could I maybe look around to see if there's something in a drawer somewhere I could put on?"

"Good Christ," I mutter, and go to my duffel bag, which is still in the corner. Pulling out a T-shirt and a pair of sweats, I go back and thrust them at her. "Here."

She blinks. "Thank you," she murmurs. I go to the couch and fling myself down, lighting a cigarette. I watch through the bathroom doorway as she carefully drapes the clothing and the towel over the shower door and gets in with her dress on. A few seconds later, the dress is flung over the door as well, and then a small hand snakes out and shoves a bra and a pair of dark panties into the sleeve.

My cock goes hard as a bat. Christ, it's not even ten in the morning yet and already I want a drink. This girl is going to drive me mad if I'm not careful.

While Isabel is showering, I pull out my phone and call Gunner. "Where the fuck are you?" I demand.

"Jesus, you're in a foul mood this morning," he replies cheerfully.

"You don't know the half of it," I rumble. "So, where the fuck are you?"

"Alix is packing a bag for the girl. I'm sending Beast up with it a little later. Rock's got me going on a run with him, Ghost and Angel."

"What's the run?"

"Taking that shipment down across the border to the Reign of Hell."

I grunt. "Good luck."

"Thanks. Beast should be up to you by mid-afternoon," Gunner continues. "I'm here at home right now. Taking off for the clubhouse in about an hour. You think of anything specific you want Alix to send up, text me before then."

"Will do." I'm about to hang up, when I remember something. "Bring up a quart of milk if you can."

"Got it."

A few minutes later, the water shuts off. I watch as the towel disappears over the shower door. Knowing Isabel is in there, wet and naked, is fucking with my head. My cock is so hard it's aching. I think back to her reaction when I told her she could get me off if she wanted to. I said it to shock her, but the look on her face — the way her breathing sped up, like it excited her as much as it scared her — it fuckin' did me in. I made sure to get my rocks off at the clubhouse with Melanie and Tammy before we went to pick up Isabel, knowing I was about to go through a dry spell. But I didn't bargain for the constant temptation that this girl is turning out to be. Who would think that an ugly fucker like Oz could produce something that looked like *that*?

The towel goes back over the shower door, and my shirt disappears. A few seconds later, so do my sweats. I can't help but notice she hasn't put her underwear back on, or her bra.

I could slip my hand under the waistband of those sweats so easily. Slide my fingers against her hot, wet pussy... make her moan for me... pull them down and sink my cock inside her...

A sharp jolt of pain singes my middle finger. Yelping, I look down and see my lit cigarette has burned down to its nub.

A few minutes later, Isabel comes out of the shower wearing my clothes. I'm flipping through channels on the TV, looking for a game to watch to keep my mind, and my eyes, focused elsewhere.

Isabel's nose wrinkles. "Do you have to smoke in here?"

"I'll do as I please," I mutter darkly.

She sighs, clearly exasperated. "When is your friend going to bring me something else to wear?"

I glance over at her with a frown. Isabel's hair hangs wet, away from her face. Her features are even more striking like this. High, elegant cheekbones, eyes that are dark and intense, even without the makeup that she's washed off. My clothes hang huge and shapeless on her. But it doesn't make her less sexy. On the contrary, my hands itch to reach underneath the fabric, knowing that she's naked underneath it all.

Angrily, I turn back to the TV. "Soon. Today."

She nods. "Thanks."

Without waiting for an answer, she pads back into the bathroom. I can't help but watch as she reaches into the mirrored cabinet, stares inside, and pulls out an old tube of toothpaste. Squeezing some onto her finger, she starts rubbing the paste vigorously across her teeth.

Sighing, I pull out my phone and text Gunner to have Alix send along a new toothbrush.

When Isabel is done in the bathroom, she comes into the living room and stands next to the chair.

"Are you going to tie me up again?" she asks.

I cut her a look. "That depends on you."

"What about me?"

"Look. Isabel." I lean forward. "We are a good twenty miles from anything. It's forty degrees outside. You're barefoot and you have no coat. If you try to run, you won't survive it. That's assuming I don't catch you. If you're not an idiot, I can let you stay untied. Are you an idiot?"

Anger flashes across her face. "No," she spits, her chin jutting.

"We'll see." I lean back and cross my arms. I've found an American football game on. Both teams are shite, but I'd rather look at them than her.

A few seconds pass in silence. Out of the corner of my eye, I see her lean down. Glancing over, I watch as she picks up her necklace, which has been lying on the floor beside her chair since last night.

Isabel comes over to the long couch and sits down on the opposite end, as far away from me as she can manage.

A few more minutes pass in silence.

"Do you like football?" she asks, staring at the screen.

"It's all right."

"You're not American," she observes.

"Irish."

"Oh."

Isabel pulls her knees up toward her chest. Her head bows down in concentration. She starts to fiddle with the necklace.

"Is it broken?" I find myself asking.

"I think I can fix it," she murmurs. "It's just the clasp."

"Why do you care so much about a damn necklace?"

"My mom gave it to me," she says in a quiet voice.

Her ma. Funny I never even thought about her having a ma.

"Where is she? Your ma."

"Venezuela." She lets out a small sigh.

"How long's she been there?"

"Three years." Isabel holds out the necklace, testing it. "It's where she was born. As soon as I graduated from high school, she left to go back and take care of her parents. The economic situation there is terrible. People have to stand in line for hours, sometimes days, to get food. And my grandparents are old, and can't really fend for themselves anymore. So, my mom has to do it for them."

I don't say anything in response. But I know what it's like not to see family for a while. How long since I've seen my own ma? Twelve years, it's been.

Jimmy would be a grown man now. The two of you'd be drinking down the pub together.

The grief hits me like a bullet, like it always does. I audibly wince, and Isabel shoots me a curious look, which I avoid by standing up abruptly.

"You want a beer?" I mutter.

"It's a little early for me," she says, amused.

"No such thing." I reach in the fridge for a cold one, pop the top, and take a long drink. When I pull the bottle away from my face, my hand is shaking.

Clenching my jaw, I shove the thought away. Like I've been doing since the day it happened.

"It's hard to imagine Oz with an old lady," I tell Isabel.

"Oh, they aren't together. Haven't been for years." She shrugs. "Honestly, I barely remember the time when they were. Mom took care of me for most of my childhood. Dad hardly ever came around. He gave her money, but that's about it. He didn't want to be a father. Especially not to a girl."

The disgust in her voice is evident. But there's also pain.

"You sure about that?" I ask, not sure why I'd be defending Oz. "He doesn't exactly strike me as the kind of guy who's good at expressing his feelings."

"Dad doesn't care about anything but his club," she scoffs. "And making money, or whatever they do, and being tough. Being the guy that everyone's too scared to mess with. Being a parent? Not on his radar."

"If he didn't care about you, he wouldn't be going to such lengths to protect you, would he?"

"Please." Isabel snorts. "Dad's become a caveman about me ever since Mom left. While she was around, he didn't have to give me a second thought. This? It's just an ego thing. He doesn't want his precious daughter defiled. That's all this is. He'd lock me in a tower if he could, but he can't, so this is the next best thing. It has nothing to do with me."

I'm about to tell her she has it wrong, but I don't know how much of the situation Oz would want me to share. Suddenly, Isabel lets out a cry of delight.

"Look!" Isabel crows, holding up the necklace. "I fixed it!"

The grin on her face is so wide and happy that for a second I forget everything I'm supposed to be doing and almost grin right back. My chest constricts, because in spite of all this shite I can't help but be happy for her that she's fixed her stupid fucking necklace and that this one tiny thing has made her so freaking ecstatic. Even though she's basically a prisoner here, and I'm in charge of making sure she stays that way.

This is bad. This is very bad.

Wanting to have sex with her is one thing. Of course I do, she's fucking hot. But I can tame that demon by jerking off. I've been fighting to keep my cock at half-mast ever since I woke up this morning, and for the most part I've managed it.

But *this* thing, this is fucking new, and it comes at me like a punch from behind. This thing where just seeing her happy about this tiny, pathetic thing makes me feel like shit for every second of how I've treated her the last twelve hours. I don't see it coming, at all. It fucking floors me.

And it's abso-fucking-lutely *unacceptable*.

What I cannot do — what I can *not* fucking do — is have any sort of personal emotional reaction or attachment to her. At all. My job is to keep her here. And to keep her safe. And the only way I can do that is by not giving a shit about her personally.

There are consequences for letting your feelings in for someone you're trying to protect. I know that for a fact. From bitter fucking personal experience.

I'm about to make some crass, offhand comment about the necklace when a loud bang from the porch jolts me out of my thoughts. Instantly, I fly up off the couch and reach to my waistband for my piece. But then I see Beast's ugly mug through the window grinning at me.

"God fucking damnit, I'll murder the son of a bitch," I rasp. Striding toward the door, I turn to Isabel. "Beast is here with your things," I say, my frustration coming out as anger. "Try anything stupid and you'll be back tied up to that chair for the duration."

9
ISABEL

The man Thorn calls Beast comes in with a large pink duffel bag. It's stuffed full, and slung over his shoulder. It's a strange image: he's one of the tallest men I've ever seen, and absolutely *massive*, with muscles that look like they're not even made of human flesh but of some hard, unyielding material. I remember his face and his deep baritone voice from before. But when the Death Devils handed me over to the Lords of Carnage, at the time I was too afraid and confused to pay much attention to him until now.

Beast sets the pink bag down beside me on the couch. Then he unties my feet from the chair and raises himself up to his full height. "Gunner's old lady said she hopes she thought of everything you'll need," he rumbles. "She said to have Thorn let her know if you want her to send you anything else next time someone comes up."

Beast is almost like a monster — like some non-green version of the Incredible Hulk. But even so, he's still being kinder than Thorn is being to me right now. I find myself wishing that he was the one in charge of me, instead of Thorn. I thought we were sort of starting to get along okay for a little bit, but right around the time I managed to fix my necklace he turned back into a surly asshole. Disappointment floods my chest for a few seconds, but then I remembered Thorn's my captor, not my friend. So I guess it's actually a blessing in disguise that he's making it easier for me to hate him.

"Thank you!" I say, shooting Beast a shy smile. I go to the couch, unzip the duffel and look inside. There's a bunch of clothing on top. I take out a women's fitted t-shirt and hold it up; it looks like it will fit me, more or less. There's a new pack of underwear, thank God, and some jeans and warm-looking socks. There's a toothbrush, and even some floss — like my dental hygiene will be my biggest worry as a captive out here in the middle of nowhere. She's even put in some face soap, and some shampoo and conditioner. I almost laugh at how thoughtful this is; it's something I'm sure none of these men would even have thought to do. I'm oddly touched and grateful to have even these small comforts. Whoever the woman is who packed this bag, I can't help thinking she must be nice.

As I keep digging down, my hand brushes something small and hard that I can't identify. I grab onto it and pull it out. A Kindle! There's even a charging cord wrapped around it. Turning it on, I see it's fully charged, and loaded with books. From the eclectic look of the library, Gunner's old lady has sent her own personal Kindle to me. Breathing a happy sigh, I send out a silent thank you to this stranger, who may have just saved me from going insane with boredom.

I get to the bottom of the bag, noting the other items that my kind stranger has packed for me, when it occurs to me that something's missing.

"Oh no!" I murmur with disappointment.

"What?" Thorn barks impatiently.

"There aren't any shoes in here."

"What d'you need shoes for? You're not going anywhere." His voice is threatening.

"Why are you being such an ass?" I fire back.

"Oh, so now I'm being an ass, am I?"

"Yes, you most certainly are!" I say hotly. "What have I ever done to you, for you to treat me like this? Next to you, my father seems like Mary Poppins in comparison!"

"Yeah, well if it wasn't for yer fuckin' father, I wouldn't be here right now, lookin' after your sorry, ungrateful hide," Thorn grimaces, irritated.

"Jesus, can the two of you stop bickering for a second?" Beast interrupts us. He looks at me, clearly amused. "You want me to ask Alix to send you some shoes the next time around?"

"Yes!" I say.

"No!" Thorn shouts at the same time.

"Fuck you!" I cry, stamping my foot at him. "Why can't I just have a damn pair of shoes?"

"I don't want you getting any stupid ideas about trying to escape."

I round on him, fury almost choking me. "I would walk over hot coals in my bare feet to get away from you!" I scream. "Shoes or no shoes!"

I can't stand it anymore. I hate being here with him. Grabbing the duffel, I fling the strap over my shoulder, flash a look of silent apology to Beast, and stomp into the single bedroom, slamming the door behind me.

Hurling myself down on the bed, I start to sob, hammering on the mattress with angry, useless fists. I hate being here, hate being so helpless and isolated and with this cocky asshole who acts like *I'm* the inconvenience, when I didn't ask to be fucking kidnapped and held captive against my will. Even Beast, who is huge and freaking terrifying, isn't acting like he blames me for all of this like Thorn seems to.

I lie there and cry out my frustrations and anger. Eventually, I hear the front door slam and the roar of an engine starting up. Once again, I'm alone with Thorn. For a second, I consider flinging open the window and running after Beast, to beg him to take me with him. But I know there's no point. Tiredly, I haul myself up into a sitting position and reach for the duffel. One by one, I take all the objects out and set them out on the bed. I stack the shirts together, and open the packages of underwear and socks. I hold up the two pairs of jeans she's included. They're a little bit short, but it looks like they'll fit, more or less. I peel off Thorn's shirt and sweats and put on a tank top, one of the pairs of jeans, and some thick, fluffy socks. The only bra I have is the strapless one I was wearing under my dress, and it's in the bathroom still. *Damn.* I should have asked Beast for a bra in the next shipment, but I probably wouldn't have been able to bring myself to say the word *bra* to him, anyway. My face flushing at the thought, I pull on a warm-looking hoodie over the tank for warmth and more coverage of my boobs.

When I'm done getting dressed, I want to just stay here in this bedroom, away from Thorn. But after I've put all of the contents of the duffel into the top drawer of the small dresser under the window, there's nothing else in here for me to do. Stupidly, I left the Kindle out in the living room on the coffee table.

Anger boiling inside me, I snatch up Thorn's T-shirt and sweats and open the bedroom door, intending to throw his clothes in his face. When I get out into the main room, he's in the kitchen, talking on the phone with his back to me. I pause in mid-throw, defeated. My dramatic gesture won't have as much of an impact if he doesn't even see it. Going over to the couch, I snatch up the Kindle. But instead of flouncing back into the bedroom right away, I decide to linger, and try to catch what I can of the conversation. I perch on the armrest of the couch pretend to start looking through the library on the device.

"... some of the brothers to stand guard... No, at this point I don't think there's any reason. What did Oz say?... Yeah. I'll be talking to him about that... Understood. All right."

Thorn turns to look at me when he's finished talking. His eyes briefly register that I've changed clothes, then flick away.

"What's up?" I ask.

"What d'you mean?"

"You were asking about my father. What did he say?"

"Club business," he mutters.

I roll my eyes. "Oh, brother. Yeah, I know that drill. Women are too stupid or fragile to know anything."

"Not that you deserve a fucking answer to that," he fires back, "but this isn't even your father's club. Why the hell would I tell you anything about it?"

"Fine," I huff. I snatch up his T-shirt and sweats from the couch where I've dropped them and hurl them at him. But since I'm sitting down I don't get enough of a windup, and they hit him at thigh level before falling limply at his feet. Thorn gives me a disgusted look and picks them up.

"Christ," he murmurs. "I'm going outside to chop some wood. We're almost out of heating oil. Don't…"

"Ugh, I *know*. Don't get any ideas of escaping." I suppress the urge to scream in annoyance. "*Seriously*, Thorn, let it *go*! Where the hell would I escape to, anyway? You said yourself I wouldn't survive it if I tried."

He flashes me a look and stomps out the front door, slamming it behind him. I take a deep breath and let it out, savoring the fact that for just a few minutes, I'm blissfully alone.

Which leaves me to contemplate a way to escape in peace.

Okay, so I have no idea where I am. And sure, I still don't have any shoes.

But, I now have multiple pairs of thick, warm socks. And a sweatshirt. And more clothes. If I layer them, I should manage to stay warm enough to stave off the cold. I just need to figure out the most logical direction to walk, and time it so I have as much time as possible before Thorn realizes I'm gone.

I can do this. I can.

All I need is a plan.

10
THORN

It's true we're almost out of heating oil, so I'll need to make a fire to keep us warm throughout the night.

What's less true is that I need to go chop wood. There's plenty of it stacked against the far side of the house. But I need to get away from Isabel for a few minutes. And some physical exertion is the best thing I can think of right now to get my mind off her and keep me from going out of my mind.

It was one thing seeing her wearing my clothes. At least that way, she was covered up more than she was wearing that tight dress we brought her here in. But now my T-shirt and sweats smell of her, meaning I can't wear them myself, unless I want a constant reminder of her naked body warming them up.

She's dressed in a sweatshirt and jeans that Alix sent her now. And it should be a relief, but it's not. Somehow she manages to make even that look good. I wish she'd just stayed in the bedroom, so I could pretend she wasn't here. Truthfully, the best chance I have of that is to keep pissing her off. The less she wants to be in the same room with me, the better off I'll be.

The loud thwack of the ax sinking into the wood is soothing, as is the rhythmic movement of my arms as I swing it through the air. A few minutes in, I start to sweat. I pull off my cut and lay it over a log, then continue chopping. The sweat soaks through my shirt, and gets in my eyes, but I don't stop. Instead I swinging harder, grunting every time the ax connects.

By the time I've chopped two cords of wood I'm exhausted, but feeling better than I have since Rock told me about this bullshit assignment. I straighten up and take a few deep breaths, enjoying the chill of the air connecting with the heat of my body. I grab up enough wood to start a decent fire. Then reluctantly, I head back to the house.

Inside, I find Isabel in the kitchen, rummaging through cupboards.

"What the hell are you doing?" I bark at her.

She rolls her eyes at me. "Looking for a can opener to kill you with," she says sarcastically. "God, Thorn, what do you *think* I'm doing? I'm trying to see what we have to eat. We never had lunch and now it's almost dinner time. I'm starved."

I want to shoot back a retort, but nothing comes to mind. Instead, I grab a beer from the fridge and watch as she moves around the room, taking stock of the groceries Beast brought. "There's a lot of meat here," she murmurs when she opens the refrigerator and peers in. "Haven't you guys heard of vegetables?"

I shrug. "Next time you can give him a shopping list." Isabel leans over to look at the bottom shelves of the fridge. I take the opportunity to stare at the way the jeans she's wearing cup her ass. My cock hardens instantly, beginning to throb as I imagine plunging it between those cheeks and taking her doggy style against the kitchen counter.

"I need to take a shower," I croak. The sweat drenching my shirt is starting to cool. I clear my throat. "I'll need to tie you up for that."

Isabel raises a brow and tilts her head at me. "Seriously?"

"Yes. No arguments. Come on."

Shaking her head, she closes the door to the fridge. Quickly, she grabs a bag of crisps on the counter and rips it open. "At least let me eat a couple of these to tide me over."

"Hurry it up," I growl. She shoves a few in her mouth, giving me a look like she wants to stick out her tongue at me. Then, casually, she walks over to the chair where she was tied earlier. Holding up her arms dramatically, she looks up at me, eyes narrowed.

"Here," she scoffs. "Since you're too scared to leave a shoeless, unarmed girl alone for even a few seconds."

I ignore her smart mouth and don't respond. I can think of about a dozen ways to shut her up, at least one of which involves her lips around my cock, but unfortunately I can't do that. Grabbing the rope off the floor, I kneel in front of her and make quick work of binding her legs to the chair. Being this close to her isn't doing me any good. I wonder if she can tell how hard I am, or that I'm working to control my breathing.

A little roughly, I slip the rope up the back and tell her to put her arms behind her, which she does without further argument. Standing up, I take a moment just to look at her. Christ, she looks good. She's completely helpless like that, and when she's not shooting off her mouth it's hard to stay angry with her. Her eyes meet mine, and for a second, I see the reflection of something I want and don't want at the same time.

Just under the fear, a flash of desire.

She wants what I want. At least, part of her does.

It's turning her on to be helpless like this in front of me. Just as it's turning me on to have her here so helpless.

Isabel's mouth opens slightly as she gazes up at me, her teeth capturing her plump bottom lip. It's an unconscious gesture, but it draws my eyes down to her mouth. I force myself to pull them back up, and they lock back on hers. Instantly, she looks away, her cheeks pinking prettily.

"I'll untie you when I'm out of the shower," I tell her, turning abruptly before she has a chance to answer. Seconds later, I'm in the bathroom, door mercifully closed. I turn on the water and peel off my sweat-soaked shirt. Unbuttoning my jeans, I unzip my fly, and my cock springs free from its painful prison. Even though Isabel's tied up outside, I almost lock the door.

Not to keep her out. To keep me in.

I've never turned down willing pussy in my life. Especially when it looks like her.

I can't believe I'm walking away from her instead of taking her to that bed and fucking the life out of her.

It's nothing to do with Oz. Him, I don't give a shit about. If he found out I'd screwed his daughter, maybe he'd have his men come after me and pound my ass into the ground. But to fuck Isabel — to hear her scream my name as she comes all over my cock — I have a feeling it'd be worth it.

No, it's not him I'm worried about. It's my club. I can't betray my president. I can't risk an alliance that the Lords of Carnage need right now.

Why the fuck can't Isabel have a face like a hyena, and a body to match? Instead of those dangerous fuckin' curves. That ass like a plump peach. Tits that are just begging me to reach out and touch them. And a mouth that was made to wrap itself around my hard cock.

Stifling a groan, I step into the shower and lean against the wall. Reaching up, I grab my pulsing hard-on and start to stroke. Oh, *fuck* that feels good. I'm already on a hair trigger, and I feel like I'm gonna go off like some twelve year-old boy seein' his first porno. My mind is full of Isabel, so full that I have trouble deciding on an image of what I want to do to her. I finally settle on bending her over the kitchen counter and taking her from behind like I was imagining earlier. In my mind she's naked, her ripe, willing ass flushed and ready for the taking. I stroke a little harder as I imagine grabbing her hips and sheathing myself inside her. My balls start to tighten, and I know I'm not going to last long. Isabel gasps and takes all of me in, warm and willing. As I thrust, faster and faster, she braces herself against the counter. Looking back at me over her shoulder, she casts me a wanton, knowing look through the curtain of her hair that sends me over the edge.

I come all at once, a massive explosion that feels like it's detonated through my entire body. It sends a blast of my load so hard against the shower wall that I actually hear it over the water. I brace myself as I shudder through the orgasm, just managing not to shout out loud with the force of it. I stand there for a few seconds, breathing heavily, until the pounding in my chest starts to slow. When I think I can stand, I grab the soap and lather up, my mind numb. Then, finally, I turn the water as cold as I can stand it, and let it wash over me for a full minute.

But even as I do, I know this was only a temporary fix for the problem I'm faced with. I'm stuck in a house alone with a woman I have to stay away from, for God knows how long. And there's no amount of cold water in the world that's going to get my mind off of how badly I want to fuck Isabel.

11
ISABEL

By the time Thorn comes out of the shower, it's already starting to get a little cold in the cabin. He emerges wearing jeans and no shirt, his hair damp and glistening.

I try not to look at his chest when he comes into the room, but since he barely gives me a glance as he goes over to his bag, I can't help but sneak a peek. He's absolutely gorgeous, easily the best-looking man I've ever seen up close before. His muscled chest and arms are lined with tattoos that move when he does, making it hard not to stare in fascination. He looks positively *chiseled*, almost as though he's sculpted of stone, but stone that begs to be touched, explored... clutched at...

The jeans hang low on his hips, revealing the top of a spectacular V and the hint of a treasure trail. Thorn is so muscular and massive, what I can see of him, that my mind immediately invents an image of what must be underneath his jeans. Between my legs, wetness starts to grow as I imagine the hot, hard length of him, how majestic he would look standing before me, with nothing concealing his naked body at all.

"… fire while you start dinner."

I blink at him in confusion. My face flames. "I'm sorry, what?" I babble.

Thorn narrows his eyes at me for a moment, cocking his head. "I said, if you're hungry, I'll work on building a fire while you start dinner."

Thorn has a dark gray shirt in his hand, which he yanks over his head as I try to recover my senses. "Uh, sure, that sounds good, thanks," I stammer. He gives me a brief nod and strides over to untie me. I'm so embarrassed from being caught thinking about him in that way that I can't even manage a sarcastic comeback. Instead, I just wait for him to turn me loose and then pad out to the kitchen without another word.

I sneak a few more glances at Thorn as he starts to stack logs in the fireplace. But I'm afraid to be caught staring at him again, so I force myself to turn away and busy myself with preparing a meal. I pull out some ground beef and buns and decide to just make hamburgers. I even find some frozen fries in the freezer that I can bake in the oven.

As I work, something about being able to move around and *do* something starts to improve my mood. I actually catch myself humming softly as I turn on the oven to pre-heat and rummage around for a pan to put the fries on. *Seriously, Izzy? I chide myself. Have you forgotten that you're being held against your will by a man who clearly hates you?*

That sobers me up a bit. But it's still a relief to not feel so miserable and afraid, if only for a little while. And I'll take anything I can get at this point. I busy myself forming patties and forget about everything but the process of making the meal for just a few more minutes.

When the oven is preheated, I spread out the fries on the pan and put them in, then start cooking the burgers. "Do you want fried onions?" I call over my shoulder to Thorn. "I can make some to go on top if you want."

All I get is a grunt in response, which I decide to take as a yes. I grab an onion from the counter and slice off a few rings to fry in some butter. It occurs to me to be slightly surprised that Thorn is allowing me to handle a kitchen knife. But as pissed as I am that I'm being held prisoner here, I know I'd never be capable of actually stabbing someone unless they were literally trying to kill me. And besides that, Thorn is so much stronger than I am, I doubt I'd even manage to get a blade close to him if I tried. And I'm guessing he probably knows that, too.

I set two places at the small round table and put out ketchup and a glass of water for me. I start to ask Thorn what he wants to drink, but then decide that I'm not his servant and he can figure that out for himself.

By the time the food is done, Thorn's got a nice fire going in the fireplace. I glance over at it in approval, but don't want to give him the satisfaction of a compliment. "Food's ready," I call to him, and sit down at the table without waiting for him. He stands up and goes over to the fridge. Opening it, he glances over.

"Beer?"

"Sure, why not?"

It makes me feel just a tiny bit of satisfaction that *he's* the one asking *me* if I want a drink. Small victories.

He comes to the table and sits down opposite me. He places a bottle in front of my plate.

"Smells good," he grunts.

"Thank you."

Thorn takes a large bite from the burger. "Tastes good."

"I can do the cooking while we're here, if you'd like," I hear myself offering. "It'll give me something to do."

He gives me a nod. "Okay. We'll eat better that way. I'm not much of a cook."

I try not to feel too pleased by the small compliment.

"Well, I'm probably not that much better," I admit. "But my mom did teach me a few things. Most of them involve ingredients we don't have, though."

"Venezuelan food?"

I nod. "Arepas. Empanadas…" At his frown, I explain. "Arepas are kind of like tacos, but with fried corn meal. Empanadas are little fried dumplings with stuff inside. Spicy." Even though the burger is good, I feel a pang of hunger for these foods that I've barely even eaten since my mom left. "Lots of corn, rice, beans. Plantains and yams." I shrug. "You'd have to try it to know what the flavors are like."

We continue eating in silence. I take a few sips of my beer, and enjoy a brief feeling of near-normalcy.

"You're not quite what I expected," Thorn says then, out of the blue.

"Oh?" I arch a curious brow. "What exactly were you expecting?"

"With a father like Oz? A pain in the ass."

I let out a bark of laughter in spite of myself. "And instead?" I ask.

"Well, you *are* pain in the ass." He looks at me pointedly. "But not quite as bad as I expected." He pauses for a beat. "Also, you have better tits than I imagined."

His words are so out of the blue that I almost choke on my mouthful of burger. Coughing a bit before I swallow, I glare at him. "I don't know whether to be flattered or pissed at that remark."

"Why would you be pissed?" He looks at me innocently, but I think I can see a gleam of mischief in his eye.

"Um, because it's a totally sexist and inappropriate thing to say, for one thing."

Thorn shrugs and says nothing, taking another bite of his burger.

I open my mouth to berate him some more, but realize I'd just be prolonging having a conversation with him about my boobs. And in spite of the fact that his words *were* totally sexist and inappropriate, they've still left me feeling uncomfortably warm.

I decide it's time to change the subject.

"How well do you know my father, anyway?"

"I don't," he shrugs. "Or hardly, anyway. I've met him a few times. I've seen him with his men. Seems like a good leader. They respect him."

I smirk. "Yeah. If you can call fear respect."

"Fear *is* respect. Of a certain type, anyway."

"I guess we'll have to agree to disagree on that one."

He eyes me. "Are you scared of him?"

"Me? No." I shake my head. "Not really. To be honest, I don't know him that well, either. Maybe not much better than you."

"How can that be? He's your father." Thorn's face is skeptical.

"I barely saw him, growing up." I take a drink of my beer, weighing how much to tell him. "When I was little, and my parents were still together, he was rarely at home. He's been the president of the Death Devils for a long time. When I was young, those were the days when he was building up the club, and that took up most of his time. My parents split up when I was about ten. I went to live with my mom. For the next few years, I only saw him every couple of months or so, if even that."

I stop to take another drink and steal a glance at Thorn. His face is unreadable. Sighing, I swallow and go on. "When I turned fifteen, my dad transformed almost overnight from being a mostly absentee father, to a strict authoritarian. He would come over to our house just to grill my mom about what I'd been doing and who my friends were. He didn't want me to do anything. He thought Mom shouldn't even let me leave the house except for school. I used to call my dad The Great and Powerful Oz," I say, laughing quietly. "Not to his face, of course. But my mom would shush me anyway, and tell me not to disrespect him like that.

"Mom went back to Venezuela three years ago, like I told you, to take care of her parents. She didn't take me with her, off course. America is the only country I've ever known." I shake my head. "Since she's been gone, Dad's alternated between being completely absent in my life to completely suffocating. Absent in the sense of giving me absolutely no direction in life, and suffocating in that he still thinks I'm fifteen and need to be monitored so my *virtue*, or whatever, won't be taken." I roll my eyes.

"Do you live with your dad?"

"Not anymore. Well, I mean, not before all *this*," I say, waving my hand in the air. "Before Mom left, she begged me to enroll in college. At first I resisted. But finally this fall, I decided she was right, so I started taking classes at a community college about an hour away. I took classes part-time and waited tables to afford rent and food."

"College girl, eh?" Thorn says, raising an eyebrow.

"Mostly to get away from my dad," I admit.

"What are you studying?"

"I don't know yet." I sigh. "And at this point, I'll probably never get the chance to find out. A month ago, Oz forced me to come home and put me under house arrest, so I had to change my classes to online." I glance around the cabin bitterly. "And now… well, I'm guessing there's no wifi here, and I don't have my computer anyway. So my semester is kind of screwed."

"Ah, don't be that way. This is only a temporary situation. You'll be out of here in no time."

"Yeah?" I scoff. "Just how is that going to happen? I still have no idea why I'm even here in the first place. And my dad is still nuts and overprotective. This could go on for months."

"In this situation, I don't think he's being overprotective," Thorn murmurs.

"Oh yeah?" I challenge, fixing him with a level stare. "Well, why don't *you* tell me what the hell is going on, then, and why I'm here? Since nobody else will?"

But he only shakes his head. "My job is to keep you safe. Oz will tell you what he wants to tell you, *when* he wants to tell you."

"Figures," I say gloomily. "You're scared of him, too."

"No," he growls. "I have a duty to my club. And this is part of that duty."

"So, what about that?" I ask. "What did *you* do to get stuck guarding me as penance?"

Thorn lets out a bark of laughter. "Oh, darlin', the things I've done, I'd be doing perpetual penance for the rest of my days. This is no penance. It's just a job."

"So…?"

He blows out a breath. "I don't know, exactly. Your father chose me."

"What?"

"Rock, my prez, tells me Oz asked for me specifically."

"That means either he trusts you, or he has something on you."

"The latter."

"What?"

"Nothing." Thorn gets up abruptly from the table, looking suddenly angry. He goes to the refrigerator for another beer. When he sits back down, the atmosphere between us has definitely chilled between us. We finish the meal in silence, and Thorn makes it clear he intends to keep it that way.

I try to pretend like I don't care, but the truth is, I'm disappointed. More disappointed than I care to admit.

12
THORN

I don't know how this girl got under my skin so quickly. Before I know it, I'm chatting with her like we're two old women having a hen party.

When she asks me why Oz chose me for the job, though, I'm caught off guard. Maybe it's because she's told me so much about her childhood. Listening to her talk about her ma and that made me think of my own ma back in Ireland. And what I left behind. Things I never think about anymore. Or try never to, anyway. Suddenly, it's all right there in the front of my mind. Along with the knowledge that if I fuck this up and the law gets involved, it's back to Ireland for me.

I crack open my beer and take a long drink. I can tell Isabel is looking at me but I ignore her. Instead, I finish my burger and reach for a second one. Chewing in silence, I will the girl to shut the hell up for the rest of the meal. But no such luck.

"So, do you really think my dad has something on you?" she asks cautiously after a couple of minutes.

"Mind yer own fuckin' business," I snap back. I expect her to cower, but to my surprise she stands firm.

"Thorn," she sighs. "Why are you acting like such a jerk? You were being sort of nice there for like half a minute. I mean, nice for a glowering asshole, but still."

"It's not my job to be nice to you," I retort.

"Your *job*!" she huffs. "Oh, for God's sake. Look. The two of us are stuck here in this damn cabin for who knows how long. I don't want to be here, and clearly you don't, either. The least we could do is try to be civil to one another. But apparently, that's way too hard for you."

"No. The *least* we could do is stop fucking playing 'getting to know you' like we're passing the time at the fuckin' bus stop." It comes out harsher than I intend, but too bad. I've let things get too friendly between us. Making her mad is probably for the best.

It works. "You know what?" Isabel snarls, her eyes flashing. "Fuck you! And fuck this. You clearly would rather eat without me, so go right ahead. I'm done!"

Slamming her beer bottle on the table, she pushes her chair back so hard it falls over. She jumps a little at the sound, but she's not about to be deterred. She storms off in her stocking feet to the bedroom for the second time today, slamming the door loudly behind her.

I get up and follow her. Turning the knob, I push it back open. She rounds on me like a little spitfire.

"Door stays open," I order.

"Fuck you!" she spits back.

I just laugh, even though part of me wants to wring her insolent neck.

I go outside to smoke and curse. I sit out on the porch for over an hour, staring daggers out at the darkness. A couple times, I think I hear movement inside. But when I go in to check on her, she's still sitting on the bed, reading her e-book. Each time, she glowers at me like she wishes she could kill me with a look.

God *damn* it, she's a pain in the ass.

God *damn* it, I want to fuck her.

This girl's got me running in circles. She's got an uncanny talent for getting under my skin. I blame myself in part, for letting myself listen to her talk about her childhood. I don't need to know anything about her. The more human she is to me — the more I know about the person I'm trying to protect — the less effective I'll be.

I'd have been able to protect Jimmy if he'd been a stranger to me. I'd have done what needed to be done, instead of standing around like a muppet.

I never thought I'd have to protect him — not like that. By the time I realized what was happening, I hesitated just a second too long. And by then it was too late.

The grief starts to seep in, cold as ice water in my veins. Angrily, I shake off the memories. I stand up on the porch and throw my now-empty bottle, as hard and as far as I can. I hear it land with a soft thud in the distance.

Then, nothing but silence. Just like before. And the tiniest whisper of the Connegut River, off in the distance. The silence reminds me that there's no one else out here, except for me and Isabel.

And my fucking cock, screaming at me about what it wants to do.

After a while, I have to go back in to stoke the fire. The kitchen table is still set from dinner. I ignore it, go set another log on the flames. Then, with nothing else to fuckin' do, I turn on the TV and stare at it with the sound off until I'm tired.

There's only one bedroom, so I'll be sleeping on the couch for the foreseeable future. Sighing in resignation, I grab a pillow and blanket from the low chest that serves as a coffee table. I wander into the bathroom to take a piss. Then I go to the bedroom to check on Isabel.

She's asleep. Lying on top of the comforter. A cascade of hair falls around her face and shoulders.

I take a step closer. Then another. My boots sound on the wooden floor, but she's too deep in to hear them. She's positioned half on her side, her breasts rising and falling evenly with her breath.

Then I just stand there. Fuckin' gobsmacked by how gorgeous she is. And how much I want to rip those clothes off her, and sink down onto the mattress next to her, and angry-fuck her until we're both spent and panting.

I've never wanted a woman like this before. I've never wanted a woman who couldn't easily be substituted for someone else. Isabel is pulling my insides to shreds. My cock aches. My chest aches. Everything fuckin' aches.

Fuck! Fuck fuck fuck!

I don't say it out loud, but inside my head, I'm screamin' it. Why the fuck did Oz have to choose me for this job? Why the fuck can't Isabel be his goddamn ninety year-old grandma, instead of his daughter?

Why the fuck indeed?

This is the worst job I've ever had in my life. Groaning, I bend forward and say her name, trying to rouse her. She doesn't stir. I say it again, louder this time. Still nothing. Finally, I reach out, touching her shoulder, and shake her a bit.

"Mmmph… what?" she mumbles.

"Wake up," I mutter.

"Why?"

Her tone is already different. She's woken up and realized where she is, and that it's me talking to her. She sounds hostile now. Guarded.

"I need to tie you up."

"What? Seriously?"

Isabel hauls herself up onto her elbow and looks at me in stunned disbelief. "You're going to tie me to the bed?"

"I am."

"I think you're taking your paranoia a bit too far."

"Not interested in what you think."

"What if I refuse?" she challenges me.

"If you refuse, I'll have to tie you down by force." My dick jumps at the thought, and a whole new series of images pops into my head to torture me tonight while I'm trying to sleep.

"I'm not scared of you!" Isabel says defiantly.

"Well, you fuckin' well should be!" I mean it, too. Right now, I'm angry enough that if I have to take her by force, I'll hurt her. I almost want her to push me. *Push me past my limits, little girl. Push me past the point where I can control myself. Do it.*

She gives me a long look, her face flushed with anger and her chest heaving. For a second, I almost convince myself she's thinking the same thing I am.

Her eyes still locked on mine, she flops dramatically back on the bed and flings her arms and legs out, like the starfish that's hanging around her neck. I grunt and go out to grab the rope. When I come back in, I start on her left leg, tying a knot securely around her ankle and then to the post. I move to the other leg. As I'm securing the rope around her right ankle, Isabel jerks slightly and lets out a whimper. I glance up at her face.

"My knee still hurts from before," she says quietly.

I remember how swollen and purple it was last night when we got here. "Sorry," I mutter in spite of myself. After that, I work a little more carefully. When I've finished with that leg, I move up to her arms. I sit down on the mattress next to her and fix her expectantly with my gaze. Isabel gives me a sour look and hands me her right wrist. I wrap the rope around it, noting that the redness and scratches from the zip ties are mostly gone now.

Isabel's skin is soft, and warm. Her wrists are small, so small I can wrap my thumb and little finger around them easily. Isabel continues to stare at me, a challenge in her eyes, as I finish the knot and play the length of rope out enough so she'll be able to move around a little.

"I don't sleep on my back," she says.

"You'll learn."

I reach across her body for her other arm. The movement brings me closer to Isabel's face — close enough that I can't help but meet her eyes for a second. They bore into mine.

Isabel licks her lips nervously.

"I'm cold," she whispers. "I'll be too cold to sleep."

Resisting the urge to swear, I stand up and reach underneath her. I lift her up around her waist and pull the bedcovers from underneath her body. The contact makes my already hard cock feel like it's going to rip out of my jeans. She wriggles a little, trying to help me get the covers out, but it just makes it worse as she brushes against me. I just manage to stifle a groan as I drop her back onto the bed and toss the bedspread and quilt over her. Standing abruptly, I cross to the other side of the bed to tie her second hand.

"There," I grit out, my jaw tense. "You'll just have to manage like that. I'll be out on the couch." I flash her a glare. "Go to sleep."

I don't wait for an answer. I can't. Instead, I go back out into the living room, turn out all the lights, and stare at the fire half-wishing it would consume me as I wait for the agony to subside.

13
ISABEL

Thorn leaves me there, bound and helpless on the bed. A couple seconds later, all the lights go out in the rest of the house, and I'm left lying there in the dark, my mind and body a confused mess after the last few minutes.

The storm in his eyes as he tied me up is an image I can't get out of my head. And I'm angry at him, too. It's not my fault he got dragged into this, and I don't know why he has to be such a moody asshole about it. But mixed up with how mad I am at him is something else, something I have a hard time admitting even to myself.

I'm... attracted to him. Like, *really* attracted. So much so that I actually wanted him to do something to me just now. The more he tied me up, the more turned on I got. So that now, lying here in the dark, my body's aflame with how much I want him to *touch* me. And I can't do anything about it.

I writhe and struggle as an ache begins between my legs. Even in the dark, I can feel the heat rising to my cheeks. I can't believe I'm even letting myself think these things. But the truth is, I can't help it. I imagine what I'd do right now if I wasn't tied up. Would I screw up my courage and go into the living room? Would I sit down on the couch next to him, and wait for him to touch me? Would I do more?

Bewildered, I realize that I'm wet between my legs. Practically soaking. I'm ready, *so* ready. For *him*.

And dying in spite of myself to know just how good it would feel if he started to touch me… and I let him.

The truth is, no man has ever given me the satisfaction I need. The few boys I've dated didn't know what they were doing, and I was too embarrassed to tell them. The only orgasms I've ever had are the ones I've given myself. And right now, I'm *dying* to slip my trembling hand between my legs. To feel my slick heat, to slide my fingers through my wetness and touch myself where I'm aching for Thorn to touch me.

Frustrated and caught up in my fantasies, I squirm with need, in vain. I have to stop thinking about it. I have to think about something else.

But I can't.

I don't know how I manage to fall asleep, but eventually I do. My dreams are a jumble of images and sensations. Thorn's face, his angry face, looms over me. Then he's kissing me, his stubble scraping the skin of my face, and it's rough and hard and perfect. I'm in his arms and I've totally surrendered to him, and I'm so happy because I can finally stop fighting, and because I know that any second now, he's going to give me what I want, what I *need*...

    The next morning, I start awake to find I'm already untied. I'm nestled under the covers in the fetal position, sunlight streaming in through the window. I was in the middle of yet another sexy dream about Thorn, and my body is abuzz with the longing that hasn't gone away since last night.

    My hands travel languidly down my body under the covers, making me shiver a little at the contact. I want to satisfy the ache, but opening one eye I see that the door to the bedroom is wide open, and I lose my nerve.

    Closing my eyes again, I lie there and revel in the warmth of the covers, wishing I could just stay here all day. And actually, I suppose maybe I could. But unfortunately, I kind of have to pee.

    I'm still wearing the same clothes as last night as I slide out of bed and go down the hall to the bathroom. I hear Thorn in the kitchen banging around. Defiantly, I close the bathroom door before he can tell me otherwise, and enjoy a rare moment of privacy as I relieve myself. I close my eyes, take a few deep breaths and give in to the reality of another day being cooped up with a man who hates me and excites me.

I finish up quickly and wash my hands, so I can leave the bathroom before he comes to check on me.

Thorn has already eaten breakfast by the time I get up, as I see from his dirty plate on the kitchen table. He's nowhere to be found when I exit that bathroom, though, so I assume he's gone outside. I find some cereal in the cupboard and pour myself a bowl with some milk. Then I sit down by myself at the table and start to eat.

He comes in just as I'm finishing up. Instead of saying good morning, he just nods. "There was coffee," he says without preamble. "But you slept so long I drank it all."

I frown. "I guess I must have been tired. What time is it?"

"It's after eleven."

"Eleven in the morning?" I squeak, and then I feel like an idiot, because of *course* he means eleven in the morning. But one corner of his mouth goes up in a reluctant half-grin. And then, even though I still feel like an idiot, I also feel just a little bit better, because maybe that's a sign he's not as mad at me this morning as he was last night.

"Yeah, that one," he says. "Gorgeous day out, by the way."

"Fat lot of good that does me," I point out. "Since you won't let me go outside."

"Sure I'll let you go outside," he replies evenly. "Knowing you're not likely to go far in stocking feet."

"Really?" I ask, hating how excited I sound. It's probably pathetic, but I *am* excited. Heck, doing anything that doesn't involve sitting on my butt or being tied to a bed seems amazingly exciting right now.

"It's cold enough you'll want to bundle up a bit," he says, but I'm already up and out of my seat. I go into the bedroom and put on three pairs of socks. I come back out in the living room and Thorn watches, a slight smirk playing on his lips, as I wrench open the door and step out onto the porch.

It's only been a day or so, but it feels like I've been locked up inside for weeks. I'm not exactly the most outdoorsy person, but God, it's so nice to feel the cold air on my cheeks. I pull the arms of my hoodie over my hands since I don't have any mittens. Then, taking a deep, cleansing breath, I walk down the steps and out into the yard.

There's not much of one, to be honest: it's mostly just a small patch of low grass. The house is surrounded on all sides by taller grass and weeds. I take a few more steps, then turn around to look back for the first time at the house that's been my prison. When we got here, of course, I had that damned hood over my head, so I've never actually seen any of this. To my surprise, it's actually sort of… *quaint*. It's the kind of place I can almost imagine people renting for a romantic weekend away from it all. The dark wood siding makes the little cabin seem warm and inviting. My God, there's even a little table and two chairs on the front porch. It would be the perfect romantic spot to have a nice cup of coffee outside on a cool morning.

I step around to the side of the house. To my surprise, about fifty yards away, there's a small river running past. It's beautiful, the cold water sparkling fresh and clean in the midday sun. I take a few more steps toward it, wishing the water was warm enough that I could jump in — even though I've never swum in a river in my life. I laugh out loud at the image, and how weirdly happy it makes me to think about it. And then I remember I'm still a captive here. And that this river, beautiful as it is, isn't meant for me.

Thorn is still in the house. I'm surprised he's not hanging over me like a hawk, watching my every move. I take a few more steps toward the river. Thankfully, it hasn't rained in a while, and it hasn't snowed yet. So the ground is hard, and fairly dry. The sun warms my face and the back of my hoodie. It's chilly out here, but really quite nice, with almost no wind. It's nice enough that I could stay out here for a long time, just watching the river. Or go for a walk along the shore.

And it's not even noon. I glance up at the sky, noticing there are no clouds at all. It will probably be like this for hours.

And Thorn isn't watching at all.

I walk a little more quickly, toward a bank of trees now. My feet protest a little at the branches and small rocks I step on, but it's not too bad. Almost without even deciding to consciously, when I get into the tree cover I start to half-jog, then to run. My gut tells me to follow the line of the river — that there's got to be another house on its banks eventually. And Thorn wouldn't expect me to go this way, would he?

He'd probably expect me to go toward a road. If he didn't see which direction I was walking, he'll never know.

He'll never know.

He'll never know.

The sentence becomes almost a mantra, a silent prayer I repeat over and over to the rhythm of my steps as my feet fly over the dried leaves and through the brush. I try to run as silently as I can, at least until I think I must be completely out of earshot of the cabin. Then, I let go and start sprinting, flying through the trees with my head down so I won't be blinded by the branches.

I've never run so fast in my entire life. My still-swollen knee sings from the effort, sending needles of pain jolting through me with every footfall, but I ignore it. After a few minutes, my breaths start to turn ragged, labored. I pump my arms and run faster. My legs fatigue as I run out of stamina, my lungs tightening, screaming for me to stop.

I hit a large rock with my right foot, wrenching my injured knee to the side, and can't suppress a yelp of alarm as I fall hard to the ground. Panting, I reach for it and try to massage it with my hands. It hurts, but thankfully it doesn't feel like anything's seriously wrong. If I wasn't on the run, I'd sit here for a few minutes until the pain goes away, but I don't have that luxury. My heart hammering, I get up painfully, favoring that leg, and continue on, limp-walking as fast as I can. The trees are getting thicker now, anyway, and it's harder to find my way through them. I duck and dodge branches as I go, snagging my hoodie on a few along the way. I'm sweating now, my hair plastered to my forehead. I want to take the hoodie off, but I'm only wearing the tank top underneath and don't want to chill myself.

I peer through the trees along the shore, trying to see whether there's any glimpse of a house, or at least a road up ahead. Thorn told me there was nothing for twenty miles. I think he told me that just to discourage me, but still, I have to be prepared. This time of year, the sun sets just after five. So I have a little over five hours until night comes, and the cold with it.

I try not to think about what it will mean if I haven't found civilization by then.

Still, the thought is enough to spur me on. I trudge through the trees, my initial adrenaline trickling away. My knee is beginning to hurt less now, but my stockinged feet are beginning to feel the cold. There must have still been some dew on the ground, as wetness is seeping through the layers, to my dismay. I curse Thorn under my breath for not allowing me shoes, but then I realize this is exactly why he didn't, and actually feel *guilty* for a second that I lied to him.

Thorn's face appears in my mind, stony and tense. If he's realized yet that I'm gone, he's probably furious right now. My stomach drops a little bit, even though it's ridiculous that I would care at all how he feels about me. *He hates me regardless,* I tell myself. *And why would I even care about that? He's just a hired thug for my father. If it were up to Thorn, this would all be over and he'd never have to see me again.* I welcome the anger that surges in me at the thought. I know I need to fuel it, that it will give me strength. *Thorn's only angry because I'm making his job harder. Well, fuck him. He doesn't care about me at all. This is enemy against enemy. May the best —*

Strong, brutal hands catch me on my left side, tackling me almost to the ground. I scream in terror, then in fury when I realize who it is. "No!" I shout as his arms fold around me in an iron grip so tight it pushes the wind from my lungs. Blindly, I try to kick at his legs, but he's on top of me, pinning me immobile before I know what's happened.

"You stupid bitch," Thorn hisses down at me, his face contorted in fury. "You fucking stupid brat."

14
THORN

I've never been angrier than I am right now in my life.

Barely able to stop myself from hurting her, I haul Isabel up by her shoulders and unleash on her. "You fucking brat! You could be killed, you know that?" I shout.

"How? How could I be killed?" she screams.

"Are you fucking kidding me? Beyond being out here in the wilderness with nothing to defend yourself?" I look around us, then back at her, my eyes wide with amazement at how goddamn stupid she's being. "What if you managed to get to a road, or a house, or a town? You're no better off than you were before, with no money or goddamn *shoes*, and no one to help you if you fall into the wrong hands!"

Isabel *laughs*, then — a crazy, half-hysterical laugh of disbelief. She yanks herself away from me and leans forward, her eyes filling with angry tears.

"This is *ridiculous*!" she yells. "*God*, Thorn, don't you see you're just part of my dad's paranoid fantasy? He thinks I'm this little porcelain doll he doesn't want to see defiled, because he thinks that would tarnish his fucking honor! He doesn't give a shit about me, or what I want, or whether I even get to have a life!"

"Your father really hasn't told you a goddamn thing, has he?" A small window in my rage opens up just for a second.

"Told me what?"

I grab her by the shoulders again, shaking her a little. Suddenly, I don't fucking care what she knows. She's disobeyed me. And her father. That's all that matters. "Look. You're being a fucking idiot," I rasp through clenched teeth. "Oz might not have told you why, or how, but you're in danger. The threat is real."

I pull her close, so that her face is inches from mine. My eyes pierce into hers, so intense that she flinches and pulls back.

"Isabel," I say hoarsely. The surprising force of my relief that she's all right is making me feel a bit sick. "Don't fucking do this again. You have no idea how dangerous this was."

"No!" she shoots back defiantly. "I don't! Why don't you tell me, so I can be terrified and won't try to escape anymore! Because if there really was something — if my father isn't just trying to keep me under wraps for a while so I'll be too scared not to obey him — then why the hell won't he just tell me what it is? Why won't *you*?"

I open my mouth to respond, but then close it again. I'm not under authorization to tell her a damn thing. And though frankly, I can sympathize with her, that changes nothing. "You're just … going to have to trust me," I grunt, shaking my head.

She snorts in disbelief and rolls her eyes. "*Trust* you? Trust *you*?"

"Trust that I have your best interests at heart."

Isabel makes a rude noise with her tongue. "That's exactly what my dad says. Well, you know what? Fuck you! I don't trust people who keep secrets from me."

"Suit yourself," I mutter. Gripping her by the shoulders, I physically turn her 180 degrees and give her back a push. "Go. It's time to head back."

I follow behind Isabel as we start to make our way back to the safe house. Thankfully, she shuts the hell up so I don't have to argue with her anymore. As angry as I am, I have to hand it to her that she made it this far in the short time she was gone. It takes us almost half an hour to make the return trip, trudging through the thick leaves and brush of the forest floor.

About halfway through the journey back, Isabel's pace slows. A few minutes later, she starts to stumble and move more gingerly, as though she's having trouble walking. Here and there, I notice she's favoring one foot or another, and wincing.

I come up beside her and glance at her pale, pinched face. "What's the problem?"

"My feet are cold," she admits softly.

I look down. Isabel's socks are soaking wet, and caked with mud and leaves. I don't know how long they've been that way.

"Christ," I sigh. "I told you not to go out like this." We still have at least half a mile to go, and at this rate her feet will be frozen by the time we get back. "Come on, I'll carry you."

"What? No!" she protests. Her face sets into a mask of determination. "It's okay, I can make it."

"The hell you can." Not waiting for an answer, I reach down and catch my arm behind her legs, sweeping her up. "Put your arms around my neck, or you'll finish the trip slung over my shoulder," I order her. I expect her to protest, but after a second she obeys without a word.

I carry her the last half-mile, trying not to breathe in the scent of her hair or look into her chocolate-brown eyes as they gaze up at me. I keep my teeth clenched, and my eyes straight ahead. When we get back to the safe house, I carry her up the front porch, kick open the door, and set her down roughly in the chair facing the fireplace. Without asking, I peel off layer after layer of soaked socks until her tiny, ice-cold feet are bare.

"Don't put them too close to the fire," I mutter. "If you can't feel them, you'll hurt yourself."

I leave her by the hearth and go find the pair of my own clean, dry socks that she was wearing yesterday. Handing them to her, I watch in silence as she puts them on. Isabel stares into the fire, her face subdued. Finally, after a few minutes, she looks up at me.

"Thank you," she says quietly.

Then, as I stand there, she stands, goes into the bedroom and softly closes the door behind her.

* * *

About an hour later, Oz calls me to give me an update. I don't tell him about Isabel's escape attempt. I don't need the grief, for one thing. And for another, I don't want to bring down his wrath on Isabel. The more I think about it, it's not really her fault she feels like she's being imprisoned instead of protected. He ought to have told her why he's doing this. In her place, I'd likely feel the same way.

"Has anything unusual happened on your end?" Oz is asking me. His voice seems more tense than usual. "Anything at all?"

"No. No sign of anything, or anyone. There's been no activity at all." I frown. "What's wrong? Is something up?"

He responds with a low growl of anger. "Last night, one of my men's old ladies was hurt, badly. She is in the hospital, and will not survive. This was meant for me. To turn my men against me by targeting their wives. Our families are at the clubhouse in lockdown."

"Fuck," I swear. This is exactly what Oz was worried about. "Do you want me to bring Isabel there?"

"No. I want her far away from this. But this proves there is every reason to believe Fowler and his men are looking for her."

"Oz," I say, frowning. "Why haven't you told Isabel about this? She thinks she's being held here for no reason. Shouldn't she know what the threat is?"

"Isabel is fragile," he says dismissively. "Knowing this would only frighten her."

"With all due respect, Oz, Isabel is stronger than you think." And she is. In spite of myself, I can't help but side with her on this one. She's not the weak little flower Oz seems to think she is. She's got a backbone of steel — even when she's being a damn idiot. She's sure as hell not afraid to stand up to me. I almost chuckle at the thought. No woman has ever gone toe to toe with me the way Isabel has. And truth be told, it's sexy as fuck the way her eyes snap and flash when she's telling me to go to hell.

"Isabel doesn't need to know the details, and that's final," Oz commands. "But if you find you're having *trouble* keeping her under control, perhaps you aren't the right man for the job."

"I'm not having trouble," I bark back. I hate being stuck here, but the thought of someone else being alone with Isabel like this makes my blood run hot. "She's safe, and she's under control. There's no problem here, Oz."

"Make sure it stays that way." Oz pauses. "And please. Be careful. If you have any reason to believe you might be in the slightest danger, it's your responsibility to procure sufficient backup to ensure my daughter's safety."

"Understood," I say curtly.

"Good. I'll be in touch tomorrow with an update. Call me at this number if anything changes."

15
ISABEL

I sit in the center of the bed, arms clasped tightly around my knees. My feet are finally warm again, but I'm still trembling.

I feel exactly like the idiot Thorn tells me I am. I can't believe how stupid and childish I was to try escaping like that, with no planning and no foresight at all. As much as I hate to admit it, Thorn probably saved me out there. I wasn't going to get much further without shoes. And even if I had eventually managed to find help, I might have suffered frostbite at the very least. I could have lost toes, or worse.

The thought of going back out there and facing him is mortifying. I can't stand to think of how angry he probably still is at me. And it's even harder because his anger is justified. He'll treat me even worse now than he has been, and I'll deserve it. As pissed off as I am at my father for shutting me away like this, it's not Thorn's fault. He's only doing his job. And in this case, I should be thankful that he did it as well as he did, or I'd probably be out there in the woods alone crying, with icicles for feet.

I look down at Thorn's socks covering my now-warm toes, and bite my lip, remembering how gentle his hands were as they took off my soaking ones by the fire. A little shiver runs through me as I think about how he carried me in his arms all the way back here. He was so strong, and in spite of the pain I found myself feeling… safe. Protected. Like nothing could hurt me as long as he was holding me. It was such a strange sensation. Except for my mother, I've never felt like anyone was really looking out for me before. Gazing up into his dark, brooding eyes, I almost wanted the trip home to be even longer, so I could stay safe and warm in his arms.

Squeezing my eyes shut, I hang my head and rest my forehead on my knees. I can't believe this. Am I actually starting to have feelings for the man who's holding me captive? I snort softly at my foolishness. I must be lonelier and more hard up for human contact than I thought. And hell, maybe all the romance novels I've been reading on that Kindle are getting to me. My mind is probably going into overdrive from lack of any other stimulation. I need to get myself together. Lifting my head, I shake it dramatically back and forth a few times to clear it. But it doesn't do much, other than making me feel a little dizzy.

"Ugh," I groan. I fall back against the pillows, my arms flailing out to my sides. I stare at the ceiling and sigh. "Iz, you're pathetic. Get a hold of yourself. This is the way it's gonna be until Oz decides he's had enough of treating you like Rapunzel. So you may as well make the best of it, and stop torturing yourself with stupid ideas."

An hour or so later, a slow, methodical thumping begins outside. I emerge from the bedroom and look out the window to see Thorn chopping wood again. He's taken off his shirt, and his strong, muscular back is glistening in the late afternoon sun. I tell myself to turn away and stop looking, but I don't listen to me. Instead, I can't help but admire how really distractingly sexy this man is. He's pretty much perfect, physically. The tattoos that line his back, arms, and chest only accentuate the perfection. I watch his hands as they grip the ax, strong and sure, and can't help fantasizing what they would feel like caressing my skin, or gripping my hips…

My skin goes goosebumpy at the thought, my nipples growing taut as my eyes flutter half-closed. There's no denying it. I *want* Thorn. I can't ever remember wanting a man like this. Of course, the few boys I ever dated in high school and after were just that — *boys*. Thorn is all man. All sex and virility. It's impossible to deny it. Even when he looks at me with his habitual pissed off glower, it just makes him all the more delicious to look at.

God, how fucked up is that?

"Good thing he hates me," I mutter to myself. I snicker sadly at how ridiculous I'm being, and finally tear myself away from the front row seat to his sexiness.

Thorn stays outside chopping for a while. I wander restlessly around the cabin, wishing for something to do. Given my current aroused state, I don't feel like opening up my Kindle when I know I'll just be picturing him as the leading man in the romance I'm reading. I don't have my phone, so I can't even waste time looking at social media. *Where is my phone, anyway,* I wonder? I vaguely remember dropping it when Dad's men grabbed me. It's probably still sitting in the parking lot of the road house, maybe crushed by now. Remembering that night makes my thoughts turn to my friend Deb. God, she must be worried sick. I've barely thought about her since this whole thing started. I feel terrible that I can't even tell her I'm okay.

Well, there's nothing to be done about that now. Pushing the thought from my head, I continue wandering around the cabin and start to snoop around a bit. I open up the kitchen cabinets one by one, searching through them more thoroughly than I did yesterday. I don't discover much that's new, except for a couple of cans of off-brand Spam in something called "pizza flavor." Grimacing, I put the cans back and close that particular cupboard. "Who are these freaking savages?" I murmur to myself in disgust.

Moving on to the living room, I open the top drawer of a side table next to the couch. There's a couple packs of playing cards, what looks like a marijuana roach, and a plastic bag of poker chips. I shrug and open the door at the bottom to see a stack of board games, some of which look like they're for kids. *Huh.* It's hard to imagine any of Thorn's MC brothers having children, but what do I know? Besides, some of my dad's men have families.

I find myself wondering if Thorn has an old lady. Or kids. He hasn't mentioned anything. But why would he say anything to me, if he does? The thought isn't a pleasant one, and I chastise myself for even caring.

I close the door and wander a few more steps, when my eye lights on Thorn's open duffel bag, sitting in the corner. Hesitating for a moment, I kneel down and carefully lift up one of the flaps to peer in: shirts, a pair of jeans, some socks that match the ones I have on. Nothing special, or interesting, and I'm too chicken to dig down and look any further. I'm disappointed there's nothing here that would give me any insight into his life.

Footsteps on the porch interrupt my thoughts. I let out a little squeak and hurriedly stand. Moving to the fireplace, I pretend to be warming myself by the fire when Thorn comes in with a load of wood in his arms.

"You not warmed up yet?" he grunts as he comes over to dump the load next to the fireplace.

"No, I'm okay," I murmur, feeling my face redden. "It just feels nice here, is all."

He glances at me for a second before turning away. "This should get us through tonight," he says, gesturing toward the wood. His shirt is back on, but sweat is already beginning to soak it through. "I need to take a shower," he grunts. "So…" He nods toward the chair where I was tied up yesterday.

"Thorn," I begin, hesitating. "I'll understand if you have to tie me up. I know I deserve it. But I just wanted to say I'm sorry about earlier. It was stupid, I know. And I know I'm lucky you came after me. I'd be out there freezing to death by now if it wasn't for you. So, well… I'm sorry. I mean, I know I already said that. But…" My eyes fill with tears. I swallow hard, feeling like a dope that I'm close to crying for some reason. "I guess I'm trying to say, I promise I won't do that again. So, you can tie me up, and I won't argue. But I wouldn't go anywhere, even if you didn't."

Thorn fixes me with a hard stare and narrows his eyes. "You know I'd be a fool to believe you?"

"I know." I swallow again and shrug. "I just wanted to say it anyway." I turn and go to sit down in the chair. "It's okay," I say, holding out my arms. "You can tie me up."

Thorn continues to look at me for a few moments without moving. Then, without a word, he reaches over to the side table for the rope and kneels down to bind my feet. I let him, placing my legs to help him, then move my hands behind the chair back so he can tie them as well. He works slowly, frowning and silent. I don't know he believes me or not, but at least I hope he accepts my apology.

When he's finished, he puts his hands on his knees and stands. His eyes meet mine, unreadable.

"I'll untie you as soon as I'm done," he murmurs softly.

Then he's gone.

16
THORN

For the second time, I explode with relief in the shower, swallowing the groan as I come hard and fast. That girl is going to be the death of me.

Afterwards, I stand under the water and try to clear my head. I don't know how much longer I can last being in the same room with her and not being able to do anything about it. I thought chopping wood could relieve some of the tension. But just being close enough to her to tie her to the chair brought all the lust roaring back.

I almost didn't tie her up this time. I actually believed her when she said she wouldn't run. Clearly, I'm going soft in the head.

But fuck, it'd be a hell of a lot easier to keep my mind off that girl if I didn't have to touch her.

I'm in a foul mood when I get out of the shower, because I know jerking off will only be a temporary fix. As I towel off, I stare at the stupid mug in the mirror and ask him why he's such a bleedin' idiot. Christ, I can't stand the sight of myself. I'm being completely undone by this girl.

I know I'm glowering like a sour fuck when I come out of the bathroom to untie her. Isabel is sitting quiet and docile in her chair. She doesn't say a word when I bend down and let her loose. She actually fuckin' *thanks* me when she's free. I look at her a little sharply, and she blushes and bows her head.

"I need a fuckin' whisky," I mutter as I turn toward the kitchen.

I'm pouring myself a shot when Isabel comes into the kitchen behind me. "I could start dinner pretty soon," she offers. "If you want."

"Sure," I reply, and leave the room with the glass and the bottle. I can't get drunk, because my job is to keep her safe, but I need something to take the edge off. I sit down on the couch and set the bottle on the coffee table. I tip the shot back into my mouth, and savor the heat of it as it goes down my throat. Exhaling deeply, I sink back and close my eyes.

"Do you want to play a game of cards or something after dinner?" Isabel calls. "I found a deck in that little table over there."

"Nah. Not in the mood." I reach up and massage my forehead tiredly. I don't want to sit across from this girl and look at her all night. But she does have a good idea about trying to pass the time. "We could watch a movie, though, if you want."

"There's movies here?" she asks, surprised.

"Sure. You see the DVD player there, don't ya?" I say, nodding toward it. "There's a bunch of them in that cabinet under the TV."

"Oh my gosh!" Isabel practically dances into the living room. "This is so exciting!"

Her face is lit up like a kid on Christmas. I can't help but laugh. She's as bored as I am here. Of course she is. This hasn't exactly been a party for her either.

Isabel plops down cross-legged in front of the cabinet and opens it up, then starts pulling out DVDSs and examining them one by one. "There's a lot of testosterone movies in here," she says, wrinkling her nose.

I snort and grin in spite of myself. "Testosterone movies?"

"Yeah," she says, giving me a wide, open smile that almost rips a hole right through me. "You know. Guys destroying things, loudly and expensively."

"Huh. Yeah. Good description of it." I raise an eyebrow, conceding the point. She nods and smiles even wider.

For a moment, we're just looking at each other. Two people sharing a laugh. It feels good.

It feels fucking awful.

I lean forward and grab the bottle. "Well, this is an MC safehouse," I say with a sour look, filling the shot glass a second time. "You're not likely to find any Jennifer Aniston movies here. So fucking deal with it."

Isabel's grin fades. I feel terrible about it, but too fucking bad. She turns back to the movies and keeps looking through them in silence. The second shot goes down my throat. I start to feel a little better. I close my eyes again and lean my head back. A few seconds later, she lets out an excited squeal.

"How about this one?"

I open my eyes and look at the case. *Die Hard*.

"Yeah, all right," I approve grudgingly.

"It's perfect! I always watch this every year at Christmas."

"At Christmas? Why?"

"Because it's a Christmas movie."

I cock my head and frown at her. "No it fucking isn't!"

"Yes it is!" she insists.

"Just because it takes place during the Christmas season doesn't make it a Christmas movie, Isabel," I say impatiently.

"It's not just that!" she crosses her arms. "It's about family, and love. John McClane and his wife are estranged at the beginning of the movie. At the end, they realize they're still in love and that's what really matters. Plus, there's Christmas stuff all over the place. It just *feels* like Christmas."

"Yeah. Guns and violence being so festive." I roll my eyes.

"John's wife is named *Holly*," she says, raising her eyebrows. "Duh."

"*Duh?*" I smirk.

"Yes. Duh." Isabel gets up. "This is the movie we're watching. By the end of it, you won't be able to deny that I'm right." She sets the movie on the coffee table. "I'm going to make dinner. You just keep living in your world of delusions."

I steal a look at her ass as she goes. My dick stirs. It's a warning signal that I need to police myself, but I'm actually feeling okay right now, thanks to the whisky. I just need to keep my distance, eat dinner and watch the fuckin' movie. It'll be fine.

* * *

"All right, so it is sort of a Christmas movie," I admit.

We're sitting on opposite ends of the couch. A half-eaten bowl of popcorn is between us, because Isabel found some in one of the cupboards and insisted on popping it. We've had dinner, I've had a third shot of whisky, and I'm now nursing a beer and congratulating myself on being mostly able to control myself in Isabel's presence for two and a half hours.

I get up and throw another log on the fire. Isabel pumps her fist in victory and says *I told you so* about a million times until I mock-growl at her to back off. She has the grace to look chastened.

As the flames start to lick around the log, Isabel stretches her arms wide and sighs. "That feels so good. I love fires."

"Yeah. They are nice. That's one silver lining to being out here in the middle of nowhere, I guess."

Isabel reaches down and pulls her hoodie over her head, revealing a black tank top underneath. It hugs her body and frames her soft breasts. I notice she's not wearing a bra. I quickly look away and take a swig of my beer.

"Thorn," she says, her eyes growing serious. "Look. I know you don't exactly like me. And I'm sorry you have to be here."

"I don't hate you," I mutter. Warning bells start to go off in my head.

"It's okay. I don't blame you. I probably would too, if I was you."

"I *don't* hate you, Isabel," I say again. I should stop right there. But like a plank, I don't. "In fact, you're not *entirely* the spoiled little brat I thought you were."

"Little?" She's amused. "I'm five foot eight!"

"You're young," I correct.

"I'm twenty-one!"

How fucked up is it that I'm relieved she's not a teenager anymore?

"That's young," I point out.

"It's old enough."

Isabel stares at me for a long moment.

Slowly, without breaking her gaze, she bites her lip.

"It's old enough," she says again, more quietly this time.

Jesus H. Christ.

My cock is instantly hard as a bat.

"Old enough to be a pain in the ass," I half-croak, pretending I don't catch her meaning.

This is the first time in my entire life I've turned down sex.

And suddenly my head is swimming with so many thoughts of what I want to do to Isabel, I'm having trouble remembering why.

Isabel chuckles softly. "My mom used to say that to me when she was mad."

"What?" I say, trying to concentrate through the fog of fucking lust.

"When I'd try to argue with her about doing stuff she thought I was too young for and I'd tell her I was old enough. She'd say, "Ees-a-bel, you are old enough to be a pain in my ass.""

"Ees-a-bel," I repeat, feeling out the syllables on my tongue. "Is that how your name is pronounced in Spanish?"

She nods.

"*Sibéal*," I murmur.

"What?" she asks, frowning at the strange word.

"*Sibéal*," I say again. "It's Irish for Isabel. Sort of like Sybil."

"Shi-BAIL," she repeats, concentrating. Her eyes lock on mine and I nod.

Something in the air shifts between us.

"What about your name? Thorn?" she asks softly.

"Thorn's just what the club calls me. My given name's Sean. O'Malley."

She smiles. "Good Irish name."

"That it is," I agree.

"Well, Sean O'Malley."

My name sounds different on her lips. No one calls me that anymore. No one in the States, anyway.

Only her.

"Well, Sibéal Mandias."

"That's a beautiful name," she breathes. "When you say it."

Her eyes are still on mine. Her lips part. I can see her breasts rise and fall as her breathing speeds up.

"Fuck," I swear softly. "Isabel."

My cock is throbbing, begging to be inside her. I can't think anymore. All my fucking willpower is gone.

"You are driving me crazy," I breathe against her ear.

"Thorn," she whispers, shivering.

Gripping her hips, I pull her against me, letting her feel my stiff, needy shaft. She gasps and writhes against me as my mouth comes down on hers.

It's over. This is happening. Fuck the rest.

17
ISABEL

Thorn's kiss is hard, animalistic, *urgent*. I feel like I'm being devoured. I moan against his mouth, almost delirious with need. I've wanted him so much, my body has been calling out for him like a beacon signaling to a ship. At his touch any thought of resisting abandons me. I'm burning for him, frantic as I clutch at his shoulders and hold on for dear life, surrendering myself to him.

As his tongue probes, insistent and demanding, Thorn's hands move under my shirt. Rough, callused fingers graze my skin. It's delicious, the best thing I've ever felt. I want his hands all over me, I want him to touch me everywhere. I want him to make me his, to mark me, bruise me, make every inch of me remember him long after this is over. He pulls me closer, and my wet, throbbing core presses against his hardness, making me gasp, and I wonder if I'm about to come just from this.

"*Sibéal*," he murmurs, his lips against my throat. I shiver as I feel the heat of his breath against my bare skin and realize my shirt is already off. His lips continue to travel down, the rough bristle of his whiskers scratching along the way, until he comes to my breast and latches onto my hardening nipple with his lips. I cry out, it's *so* good, it's never felt like this before — not even when I'm alone and imagining some unknown fantasy man who would know how to make me feel. But Thorn *is* that man and he knows *exactly* what to do, and then I'm crying out again, my arms locked around his neck as he teases and torments me. My hips writhe and buck against his hard shaft, and he moves to the other nipple, licking and biting the taut bud, and then something snaps inside me and I'm already coming, shaking and calling his name helplessly as I cling to him.

I'm still lost in the fog when I feel Thorn pick me up and carry me across the room. He strides into the hallway and then into the bedroom, setting me down on the bed. I open heavy-lidded eyes to look at him and see he's pulling off his shirt and stepping out of his jeans. His heavy, thick cock springs free, and I draw in my breath and just stare at it for a second because it's huge and *gorgeous*. I didn't even know that was possible but it is, and God, I can't wait for him to be inside me. My lips parted, I look up at Thorn's face. His eyes are dark, hungry. He leans over and yanks off the thin yoga pants I'm wearing, then spreads my legs apart, and before I know what's happening he's between my legs and plunging his tongue deep inside me. I cry out again as he licks my juices, teasing my already sensitive nub into submission. I gasp and writhe, my knees falling further apart, and I can feel another wave building inside me, stronger this time, powerful and uncontrollable. My whole body tenses, and seconds later, I explode again, gasping with the force of it.

This time, when my orgasm starts to subside, I open my eyes to see Thorn towering above me. There are no words between us as his gaze locks on mine. We haven't spoken at all, only our bodies communicating with flesh and heat and need. He kneels between my legs. Hardly aware of what I'm doing, I reach down to take his enormous shaft in my hand. Thorn groans, his eyes half-closing as I squeeze him and stroke once, twice. Then, in one swift movement, he pins both of my arms above my head. With his other hand, he guides the head of his shaft against my slickness. I inhale sharply, loving the heat of him against me. Then, grabbing my hip, he pushes inside.

I freeze at first, and a soft whimper breaks from my lips. He's so large it's painful for a second, but I want him so badly that I arch toward him and beg him with my eyes to continue. I need him like this. I *need* him.

Thorn begins to thrust into me, fast and hard. His lips graze my sensitive nipples, my neck, my lips. He's like a man possessed, taking what's his, and I rock upward to meet him. Thorn increases the pace; his shaft slides deliciously against my clit with every thrust. He fills me deeper and deeper every time, and I can't get enough, I've never wanted anything more than I want him, and this. Once again, I feel myself start to climb higher and higher as a third orgasm approaches, and I can tell Thorn can feel it too from the way his eyes are burning into mine. His rhythm increases, growing erratic and jerky, and as I reach the top and shatter around him, he shoves deep inside me one final time, then pulls out and releases himself with a deep groan all over my stomach.

I'm clutching the bedsheets, drawing in ragged breaths, my heart pounding so hard in my chest I can hear the blood rushing in my ears. The mattress sinks a bit, and Thorn bends down and grabs his shirt from the floor. Gently, he wipes his hot seed off the skin of my stomach, then tosses the shirt away and eases himself into the bed. I move toward him, nestling against his chest for warmth. For a second, he freezes. Then I feel him reach up and begin to stroke my hair.

"Thorn," I whisper quietly. Just to say his name.

My captor.

I don't want to think about that right now.

I don't want to think about anything. I just want to be with him.

I just want this.

Again and again.

* * *

Thorn touches the starfish hanging around my neck.

"Why a starfish?" he asks.

I nestle closer against him, pulling the covers up around me. We've been lying in bed for about ten minutes now, not talking. I actually thought he'd fallen asleep.

"My mom knew I spent a lot of time feeling out of place when I was a little girl," I tell him. "I didn't have a lot of friends. My family wasn't exactly normal, white-picket-fence material. And having a dad who wasn't around much made it worse." I reach up to finger the small gold pendant. "She thought it was symbolic or something. An animal that's at once a star and a fish. Both sky and sea. Adaptable." I laugh softly. "Funny, to me it felt more like the symbol of a fish out of water. Not comfortable in either place. But I loved it anyway. And when I wear it, I always have a piece of her with me. Which is nice especially now, since she's so far away."

"Is she coming back, or will she stay there?"

"She'll come back after my grandparents are gone, I think." I sigh. "But that could be a long time. And of course, I can't exactly hope for her to come back, because of what I'd actually be hoping for."

I feel him nod. "I see your point."

"Can I ask you a question now?" I say. "Since you got to ask me one?"

Thorn's muscles tense for a second, but then I feel him relax a little. "I suppose that's fair," he concedes.

"Why did you leave Ireland?"

He's silent for a few moments. "It's a long story," he eventually says in a low voice. "But the long and short of it is, I was responsible for keeping a family member safe. I didn't. So I left."

"Have you ever been back?"

"No."

"Do you *want* to go back?"

He pauses a beat. "I can't want to go back," he says slowly. "Because of what I'd actually be wanting."

I'm silent, realizing how he's worded his explanation to echo mine. Sensing he doesn't want to say more, I don't press it. Instead I lie there with him, wondering what could have happened to make Thorn leave his family, to make a new life here.

"I should probably go check on the fire," he murmurs. "If we —"

Thorn freezes, his whole body going rigid.

"What?" I ask, but he tightens his grip around me.

"Sshhh," he whispers, raising his hand in a silent command.

I frown and prop myself up, trying to figure out what he's listening to. About five seconds later, I hear it: a low rustling coming from outside.

"Someone's out there," he rasps.

I want to ask him if he's sure it's not an animal, but I'm afraid to make a sound. And besides, something tells me Thorn knows what he's talking about. Noiselessly, he slips away from me and out of the bed. Crouching low, he pulls on his pants, staying clear of the window. I just glimpse the butt of a pistol before he slips it into the back of his waistband.

Thorn leans in close to me. "Stay here," he whispers. His face is deadly serious. "Don't move. Don't turn on the light. If anyone comes, get under the bed, quick as you can. I'll be back."

I nod, my eyes wide and terrified. I know instinctively that Thorn wouldn't be acting like this if there wasn't something very wrong. And as afraid as I am right now, I trust him to protect me.

I just hope I can trust him not to get hurt himself.

18
THORN

I glide across the floor of the living room holding my boots in my hand, careful not to make a sound. When I get to the front door I pull them on, then move carefully so I can see through the window without being seen myself. There's no one there.

I quietly move to the front window in the living room to confirm. Nothing there, either. At least, not that I can see.

Slowly and silently, I open the door and slip out, then close it again. The porch is half-lit by the almost-full moon. I back into the shadow, regulating my breathing as well as I can. Leaning around the corner, I look around one side of the house, and see nothing. This side's in shadow, as well, so I lower myself to the ground and get into a crouch. My left hand reaches back to pull out my Sig Sauer. The night air is chill, but I barely feel it with the adrenaline pumping through my veins. I've never been much of a one to feel panic or dread in these situations. I grew up in a world where danger was a constant, so I learned to live with it early. The feeling I get is more of a sick excitement — the excitement that comes from knowing you're about to engage in the most basic of human instincts at the core level. The instinct to survive.

But this time, there's a thin thread of worry weaving itself through the anticipation. Because Isabel is inside, and she's naked and alone. If I don't get whoever is out here before he gets to her, she could be hurt, or killed.

I can't have that.

Moving into the shadow around the right side of the house, I continue around to the back, looking behind me often with my gun raised and ready. My ears are scanning for sounds, attuned to the slightest noise, but all I hear is the quiet slip-slip of my boots in the dry grass.

It's too dark to see footprints or indentations in the earth. The tree line is fifty feet or so away from the house. All I have to go on is instinct, my ears, and what little I can see.

Then, suddenly, I hear it: a small rustling behind me, followed by the merest creak. The bastard is going for the front door.

Quick as I can, I turn around and hurtle around the corner, vaulting up to the porch. I tackle the man before he has time to register I'm there — the element of surprise is all I have on my side. In my peripheral vision, I see one of his arms rise up, and I block it just as a slicing pain nicks into my bicep. Reaching up with my gun hand, I crack him across the face with the Sig Sauer, then knock the knife out of his hands before he can sink it any deeper. The pain stuns him for a second, just long enough for me to punch him again, a solid uppercut that snaps his head back. He lands heavily on the porch, the wood groaning under his weight.

I expect that to be the end of it as I rise to my feet with the gun pointed at him, but the fucker surprises me by kicking out with his legs and getting my right foot out from under me. As I start to fall, just before my left foot leaves the ground, I manage to get some purchase and rotate my body so I land with my right elbow connecting solidly with his groin.

The cunt yowls like I just cut off his dick. He doubles over, nearly folding in half. I take the opportunity to punch him in the jaw one more time with the Sig, hearing a crunch as something breaks — probably his nose and a couple of teeth. I quickly reach forward to wrench one arm behind him. He howls again and screams, "Fuck!" at which point I pull up sharply on the arm, feeling something give in his shoulder. Then I swing him around so he's on his stomach, and plant a knee hard in his back.

"You fucking yell like that again, I'm gonna put a bullet through your skull," I hiss, my face close to his ear. The cunt grunts and writhes, but he must believe me since he does what I say.

"Is anyone else gonna come out of the trees and join us?" I hiss. When he doesn't immediately respond, I yank up on his arm again. He swallows a yelp and shakes his head frantically. "You know if you have friends out there, I'll have to end you so I can take care of the rest of them. Better tell me now."

"There's no one!" he gasps out.

My knee's pushing on his lungs so he's having trouble breathing, but I don't fucking care. I cock the pistol and aim it at his head. "You'd better not be lying, you cunt. Anyone who shoots me right now is about to shoot you by proxy."

He shakes his head back and forth convulsively. There's no guarantee he's telling me the truth, but I think if he had anyone out there, they'd be coming at me right now. Still, I keep an eye on the trees as I interrogate him.

"Who sent you?" I growl angrily. "Was it Fowler?"

Cunt hesitates a second, which is a second too fucking long. I grab his hair with my pistol hand and use it to slam his head down on the boards. "*Who. The fuck. Sent you?*" I growl into his ear, my voice cold as steel.

I have to hand it to the piece of shit — he's loyal to whoever his boss is. Loyal, and bloody stupid. I yank his head back again until I'm just short of breaking his neck, and stare into his wild, frantic eyes. "You know I'll fucking kill you," I say conversationally. "If you're afraid of your boss killing you too, isn't it better to take yer chances and disappear?"

"I can't disappear from him," he rasps, his voice thick with fear. "He'll find me, no matter what. And he won't be quick about killing me."

Fuck it. This one isn't about to talk. But the fact he's not denying it's Fowler tells me everything I need to know.

I let go of his hair and pull back, keeping my knee on his spine.

Then I shoot him in the head, execution-style.

Moving quickly, I go through his pockets. I find a Beretta .9 mm and a thin wallet, both of which I take, and a phone with only one number in it. I stand up and stare at the number for a few seconds to memorize it. Then I smash it to bits with the heel of my boot. I scan the darkness quickly, making sure I don't hear any more movement before I shove the Sig back into my waist band. Turning, I reach for the handle of the front door, but a thought stops me. Looking down at the mostly-headless body in disgust, I set the dead cunt's gun and wallet on the porch railing and grab him by the boots, hauling him off the porch and into the darkness. Isabel doesn't need to see any of this.

I reach back onto the porch for the smashed phone and toss it beside the body. There's blood and brains spattering the floorboards, but maybe I can keep her from looking at it.

I pocket the wallet and toss the gun under the porch. Then I run back inside the house. When I get to the bedroom, Isabel's nowhere to be found.

"Isabel!" I yell, hearing the panic in my voice.

"Thorn!" comes a plaintive, muffled cry.

For a horrible, sickening second, a flashback makes me weak in the knees. My stomach churns. Then, realizing she's under the bed, my heart starts hammering in my chest. Relief floods my veins so quickly I feel dizzy for a second.

"Isabel," I rasp urgently. "Come on. We have to go. Now."

A small, trembling hand appears. Then the cascade of her chocolate-brown hair. I just barely resist the urge to pull her out, knowing I'll hurt her. Instead, I kneel and wait to help her up. She's still naked, and trembling visibly.

"I heard shots. I didn't know…" her voice breaks. Tears fill her eyes.

"Shh, it's okay."

With a strangled cry, Isabel flings herself into my arms. I hold her tightly for a long second, stroking her hair and murmuring her name against her ear. She clings to me, then takes a deep, shuddering breath and pulls back. Her wide, terrified eyes meet mine, and then slide down to my arm.

"You're hurt," she breathes in horror.

"Not badly," I grunt. "Come on, get up. Pack your bag. We need to leave. *Now*. Hurry."

I want to sit here and hold her until she feels better, but there's no time. I stand, and pull her up with me. She's still looking dazed, almost paralyzed. "*Sibéal*," I say sharply. Startled, her eyes meet mine again, and then she blinks and nods. "Okay," she whispers, and immediately goes to the dresser and begins pulling out her clothes.

Isabel doesn't ask questions or hesitate as she throws on a T-shirt and jeans, then starts stuffing the rest of her things in her bag. *Thank fuck.* Striding into the living room, I take out my phone and punch in a number. My prez answers on the third ring.

"Rock. We have a problem. I'm leaving Connegut with the girl. There's a body here that needs to be taken care of. We have to go to ground."

"Understood," he grunts. "Everything okay?"

"For now." I grab my own bag and start throwing things in. "One of Fowler's men came snooping. We'll go somewhere to get out of sight for the night. I'll check back in tomorrow once I decide what to do."

"You call Oz?"

"Not yet. I'll do that later, once I've got the girl out of here."

"Be safe, brother."

"Will do."

I end the call and pause, taking a moment to look around the room. The wound on my arm is bleeding enough that I should cover it until it stops. I go to the kitchen and find a dish towel, then open a drawer and take out some duct tape. I do my best to wrap it, taping it tight to slow the blood flow. I finish packing my bag, but just as I'm about to close it I remembering something. Going into the bathroom, I open the small linen closet and reach up to the top shelf. Back behind all the towels, I pull out the small purse Isabel was carrying the night she came to me. I toss it into my bag along with the rest of my things.

When I've zipped the duffel and made sure I have everything I need, I call to her.

"Coming!"

Isabel comes into the living room, carrying her bag.

"You ready?" I ask. She nods. "Good. Let's go."

"On foot?" she asks uncertainly. I look down and remember she has no shoes.

"Ah. No, darlin', not on foot." I manage a grin. "We have a car hidden not far away. It's only about five-hundred feet or so from here."

"We do?" Isabel's mouth curve into a crooked smile. "You mean, I could have driven out of here instead of trying to walk out?"

"Only if you'd found the keys," I chuckle. Strange that even as dangerous as things are, Isabel's making jokes. My brave girl. "Which you wouldn't have."

"Where did you hide them?" Her eyes twinkle.

"Ah, no," I grin, taking her by the hand and leading her toward the door. "A man needs his secrets, after all. Now come on. Enough standing around."

"Thorn," Isabel says, her face growing sober. "What's going on? Who was out there?"

"I'll tell you everything once we're out of here," I promise her. "For now, no more talking. Follow me, as quick as you can. And don't make any noise, just in case."

19
ISABEL

On the way out the door, Thorn covers my eyes with his hand. I think he's going to blindfold me again, but as soon as we're off the porch, he takes the hand away and grabs mine instead, pulling me toward the trees with him. I do my best to keep up with him in my stockinged feet, and hope he's telling me the truth about it not being far.

I can't see a thing, but Thorn is sure-footed and swift. He keeps me close to him so all I have to do is follow in his footsteps. Soon, we come to a small clearing. Just as he said, there's a car here — a mid-sized SUV that's probably dark blue or black. He hits a button on a key fob and the lights go on, then goes to the back of the car and opens the hatch to throw our bags in. He slams the door and nods for me to get in on the passenger side. I do as he says without question.

I barely have time to buckle my seatbelt before the engine roars to life. Thorn throws the SUV into drive and presses down hard on the accelerator. The action throws me back against the seat. I stifle a yelp and clutch at the armrests as he barrels through the grass, dodging trees and rocks as though he knows the path out like the back of his hand. I try to relax, but the events of the last fifteen minutes have left my nerves raw and on edge. Instead, I concentrate on taking deep, slow breaths and staying quiet. I don't want to make Thorn's job worse by freaking out or hyperventilating or something.

A couple minutes later, we drive down into a ditch, then back up again, and then suddenly we're on a paved road. Thorn turns right and floors it. The SUV roars and accelerates rapidly, until we're going so fast I'm afraid we'll hit an animal in the dark night. But one look at his focused, determined face, and I start to calm down. Just looking at him — knowing he's right here beside me — makes me feel safe, in spite of everything.

I can't stop the half-hysterical giggle that bubbles up at the thought. Thorn shoots me a look, one thick brow going up. "This is funny to you, is it?" he growls, but a corner of his mouth twitches in amusement.

"Not exactly," I murmur, smirking back at him.

"Christ, but you've got a twisted sense of humor, girl." He shakes his head in mock exasperation and turns back to the road.

I sit quietly for a few minutes, letting him drive. "Where are we going?" I finally ask.

"Someplace safe. The safe house is compromised. We can't risk going back."

"I heard… a gunshot," I whisper. The fear threatens to return, but I push it away. "I thought you were dead."

"Not me," he says, shooting me a tight grin. "I'm harder to kill than that."

"Thorn. What happened out there? Who was it?"

In the low light of the dashboard, I see his jaw tense. I'm afraid I've asked too much. But then he sighs angrily.

"Fuck it," he mutters, half to himself. "After this, you deserve to know what's going on. I'll tell you, Isabel. But right now, let me focus on driving and thinking about where to take us for the night."

Thorn tells me to get some rest, so I doze off in the passenger seat. I don't know how long we drive, or even which direction we go, since I never knew where we were in the first place. It's still dark when Thorn wakes me up and tells me we've arrived. Opening my eyes, I see we're at a small, dingy-looking motel in the middle of nowhere. Thorn tells me to wait for him in the SUV. He locks it with his key fob and strides toward the motel's office. I watch him go and try not to count the seconds until he's back.

When Thorn returns, he unlocks the car again and climbs into the driver's seat. "We're at the end, there," he says, lifting his chin. He pulls the SUV to the edge of the lot and shuts it off again. I open my door and slide down off the seat onto the gravel below. By the time I move around to the back, he's got my bag as well as his slung over his shoulder. "Come on," he rumbles.

Thorn walks me to the door of our room and sticks the key into the lock. A stale, musty smell hits me instantly. I wrinkle my nose, but don't complain. We both have worse things to think about right now than a less-than-excellent place to sleep for the night.

When Thorn flips on the light, I take in the smallish, dingy room. There's a rickety table with two chairs by the door, and one double bed with a quilted cover. I risk a quick glance at Thorn, but he's already setting our bags on the table and pulling off his leather cut. He runs a hand over his face, raking it through his hair. I look over at the digital alarm clock by the bed and see it's after two in the morning. For the first time I realize how tired he must be.

"Go ahead and use the bathroom first," he tells me.

I don't argue. I pad across the dirty-looking carpet and push open the door at the back of the room. The switch by the door fills the tiny space with cold fluorescent light. I blink against it, turning my face away from the fixture, and shut the door. I do my business, then run some warm water and quickly wash my face, drying it with a small but thankfully clean-looking towel.

When I get back outside, Thorn is sitting at the table in the single chair.

"It's late," he grunts at me. "Get some sleep. I'll stay up and stand watch just in case."

"But Thorn," I begin. "You've had even less sleep than I have." I blink a couple of times and frown. "I could take a shift, and wake you up if…"

"No. Sleep."

"But…"

"Woman, do as I say!" It's a command that brooks no argument.

Anger flares in me. I open my mouth to shoot him an indignant retort. But then I notice again how tired his face looks, and realize I'd just be making things worse for him. I can complain about his Neanderthal behavior later, when he's had some rest.

"Okay," I say meekly. "But remember you still owe me an explanation of what the hell's going on."

"Tomorrow," he barks. "Right now, go to sleep."

I move over to the bed and pull the cover to the side. The sheets *look* clean, but I'm not convinced they are, given the state of this room. I decide I'm tired enough to just sleep in what I'm wearing. I lie down on the bed, fatigue already overtaking me, and close my eyes.

"Thank you, Thorn," I whisper.

He doesn't respond.

20

THORN

The minutes and hours pass.

I sit in the dark, the Sig Sauer on the table next to me. The curtain's mostly closed, except for a small opening for me to see through.

I stare into the darkness. And tell myself over and over what a fucking idiot I am.

I never should have fucked Isabel. I can't believe I let being isolated with her at Connegut get to me like that.

It was only because I was there with her twenty-four seven, and no escaping her ripe, lush curves.

It was only because she was there every second, her body practically begging me to taste it.

I've risked my club's alliance with the Death Devils by fucking her.

But more than that, I've risked her safety.

I almost let her get taken by Fowler's men back there. If I hadn't been following my cock, that dead fucker never would have gotten as close as he did.

Before I can stop it, Jimmy's young face appears in my mind, his eyes on me in a silent reproach.

Jimmy. I was supposed to protect him, too. And because I loved him like a brother, I let my emotions get the better of me. I hesitated just a second too long.

I can't afford to have any emotions where Isabel is concerned. My job is to keep her protected and out of danger. But goddamnit, being around her is clouding my judgment. It's a special kind of torture to be cooped up with a girl like that, trying not to look at her big brown eyes and her luscious fucking ass. Jesus, not a jury in the world would convict me for wanting her. But as much as I hate to admit it, my feelings for her go beyond just a desire to fuck her.

I think I might be falling for her just a little, too.

I must be the biggest fucking plank in the world.

I stare out into the night and call myself every name in the book. I tell myself what happened with Isabel tonight can't happen again. I've got to get my dick under control. I've got to remember I've got a job to do, and I can't let anything — or anyone — stand in the way of that.

The next morning, as soon as it's light, I slip out the door and ring Oz. As usual, he answers on the first ring.

"Do you never sleep?" I ask him.

"Rarely." There's no trace of humor in his voice. I get the feeling Oz is not the joking type. "To what do I owe the pleasure?"

"To the fact that someone found our safe house last night. One of Fowler's men. He was coming for Isabel. I ended him."

Oz lets out a stream of expletives. I'm impressed. I've never actually heard him show emotion before.

"Where's the body?" he finally asks through clenched teeth.

"The Lords are taking care of it. There'll be no trace."

I tell Oz the number that was plugged into the burner phone I found on the body. He takes it down without a word.

"Where are you now?" he asks.

"I think it's best if you don't know." I glance toward the door to the motel room. "Oz. How the hell would Fowler's man have found us? You didn't know our location. Most of my club didn't know where we were."

"I don't know."

Anger starts to boil up inside me. "I have a hard time believing that, Oz."

Silence.

"You're not being straight with me," I bark. "God *damn* it, Oz. How the hell do you expect me to protect your daughter without all the information?"

He hesitates. "I believe… there may be a mole in my organization," he says at last.

It takes all the strength I have not to smash my phone into the wall of the building. "Are you fucking kidding me?" I hiss. "And how long have you known this?"

"I haven't known. I've suspected." He pauses, and when he continues, his voice is sharp enough to cut glass. "And unfortunately, I do not know who it is. But when I find out, he will pay."

"Fuck," I snarl. I consider Oz's words. If Fowler's got one of the Death Devils talking, it stands to reason whoever it is told him someone in our club was protecting Isabel. All I can think is they managed to follow Beast to the turnoff for the safe house, and Fowler sent one of his people to check it out.

I'm just lucky they only sent one man. More than that, and I might not have been able to get Isabel out in time.

If I'm right, that means the Lords can't help us anymore. We can't call for help from anyone. I'm on my own to keep Isabel out of harm's way until this is over.

"We're going to ground," I tell Oz, finishing the cigarette I'm smoking and grinding the butt to a pulp under the heel of my boot. "The only way I can keep your daughter safe is to take her somewhere none of you knows about. Not you, not your club, not the Lords."

Oz weighs my words. "Yes."

The tension in my back loosens. Because I wasn't taking no for an answer.

"I'll be in touch tomorrow. Not this number. Watch for my call."

I hang up before Oz can reply, and power off the phone. I'm fucking filled with rage that he didn't tell me all this before. But I push it down because I have to be focused. I need to be clear in my thoughts.

I push open the door to the motel room. Isabel is sitting up in bed, her hair a mess. My cock jumps as I imagine fisting my hand in it.

"Was that my father you were talking to?" she asks in a sleepy voice.

"Yeah."

"Are you finally going to tell me what's going on?" she yawns.

"Breakfast. Let's find breakfast first. I'll tell you when we're eating."

"I don't think they'll let me in like this." She points to her feet.

"Ah. Good point. We'll stop someplace to get you shoes beforehand. I need to make a purchase myself."

Isabel gets out of bed. She comes to stand beside me and starts digging in her bag. She's close enough that I can feel the bed-warm heat of her, and I turn my back so she won't know how hard I am for her.

I sit down and wait until she's through in the bathroom. Then I go in and take a piss, and brush my teeth. When I'm finished I come back out and zip up my duffel. "Ready?" I ask.

"Ready," she nods.

I toss the room key on the table and we leave the motel. In the SUV, I turn left onto the road we came in on, in the direction of the next town. It turns out to be a medium-sized place, big enough to have a Wal-Mart and a string of chain restaurants along the highway. I pull into the Wal-Mart and park the car close to the door but off to the side of the lot.

"What's your shoe size?" I ask Isabel as I reach for the door handle.

"Why can't I come in with you?"

"You said yourself. You don't have any shoes."

Isabel snorts. "If there's one place I can think of where people won't bat an eye that I'm in stocking feet, it's Wal-Mart."

We go in together, and she's right — no one even looks twice at her. We go to the shoe department and I wait as she picks out a few different pairs of trainers and tries them on. She finally chooses one, and laces them up as I stand there scanning the store for any strange activity. When she's finished, she picks up the box to take with us. "Okay, I'm good."

I lead her to electronics and grab a couple of burner phones. Then we head to the cashiers to pay. By the time we're walking out the door, Isabel's stomach is growling audibly.

"Looks like we'd better get you something to eat," I say dryly.

"I'm starving," she confesses.

I drive us to the first chain place that serves breakfast. Isabel orders an omelet and coffee. I get eggs, bacon, and toast.

"So," she says when the waitress walks away with the menus. "Are you finally going to tell me what's going on?"

"Are you sure you don't want to wait until you've had something to eat?"

"No," she replies firmly. "I'm sick of being kept in the dark, Thorn. It's scarier than just knowing the truth."

I lean back in the booth tiredly and take a swig of coffee. The sleepless night I just spent is starting to get to me. "All right," I nod. "Where do you want me to start?"

"How about with who that man was last night at the cabin, and what he was trying to do to us?" Isabel's chin trembles for a second, but she sets her jaw bravely.

"I'm not a hundred percent sure," I sigh. "But it's likely he'd been sent by a man who's out to destroy your father."

"Destroy him?" Her face turns concerned, but not extremely so. Isabel is clearly the daughter of an MC president. She's used to Oz being in danger.

"Yeah. I don't know what the disagreement is between them. Oz never said. But what he told me is that Fowler — that's the name of the man — likes to get at a man slowly. Indirectly. By going after his loved ones first. Family." I pause a beat and look Isabel in the eye. "Especially the women."

Isabel swallows. "Oh," she says in a small voice.

Our food comes, and I continue to talk. I avoid some of the details that Oz told me had happened to other women Fowler came after. They're likely to scare her to death. All the same, her face grows pale as I talk, but I force myself to keep going. After all, Isabel asked me. And at this point, I'm through hiding it from her.

"So, all of this is real?" she asks. Her voice is devoid of expression, but I can still hear the fear she's trying to mask. "It's not just the product of my father's overactive imagination?"

"Hardly. This is very real. And you're in a lot of danger."

"And you, by extension."

"Maybe." I shrug.

"And my father asked your MC to protect me instead of his… because he wanted me kept away from anyone with a direct connection to him?" she guesses.

"That's right."

She sits for a moment, digesting this information. "So…" Isabel picks at her half-eaten omelet with her fork. "How did they find us?"

"Oz thinks there's a mole among the Death Devils. Someone who found out that Oz asked the Lords of Carnage for protection for you, and fed the information to Fowler." I push down the violent thoughts of what I'd like to do to whoever that motherfucker is. Oz had better find him, and make him pay, or I swear to God I will. "Fowler might have had people tailing the members of our MC. Looks like they got lucky and followed one of the right ones."

"Beast?"

I nod.

We finish our breakfast mostly in silence. Isabel stares down at her plate and doesn't manage to eat much more. When she's finished her coffee, I toss a couple bills on the table and we get up. Isabel has to go to the bathroom, so I come with her and stand watch outside the door, just in case.

When we're back in the car, Isabel is more subdued than I've ever seen her. I don't know if she's just trying to take it all in, or if she's frightened, or if she's angry. Maybe a little of everything.

I turn the key in the ignition, stifling a large yawn. Isabel blinks, snapping out of her reverie, and looks at me.

"I can drive, if you want," she offers.

"No. I'm driving."

"What, do you think only men are good drivers?" she smirks.

"I'm driving," I say again, louder this time.

Isabel rolls her eyes. "Fine, caveman."

The fact is, as tired as I am, there's no way I could be a passenger right now. I'm much too antsy. Driving will give me something to focus on. A way to think out our next steps.

I pull out of the parking lot and back into the snarl of chain fast-food places, auto parts stores, and fuckin' nail salons. As I turn onto the highway to head out of town, Isabel speaks up again.

"Where are you going to take me?" she asks.

I turn to look at her.

"Honestly?" I say. "I don't have a clue."

21
ISABEL

We drive all day. Thorn doesn't talk much. I let him brood, or think, or whatever it is he's doing as he clutches the steering wheel and stares out at the road. We stop for gas and supplies, stocking up on prepared sandwiches, chips, and other road trip foods too so we won't have to stop for lunch.

Thorn keeps the SUV bearing west for a while. Then at some point we turn north. I try to make a joke and ask him why he didn't choose a direction that would take us someplace warmer, but it falls flat. Thorn just emerges from wherever his brain has gone, and furrows a brow at me. Sinking down in my seat with a sigh, I look out the window and leave him to his thoughts.

That night, just as the sun is setting, we turn onto a highway that runs along a large body of water to our left. Thorn seems like he's got a destination in mind now, but when I try to ask him about it he waves me off. We pass a bunch of lodges that look like they're geared toward summer lake tourists. Finally, we pull off at the very last one, and Thorn drives up to a small cabin that says *Office*.

"Is this where you were going all along?" I ask him quizzically.

"No," he answers. "I came up with the idea a while ago."

"Have you ever been here before?"

"I have not." He opens the car door. "Let's hope we've come to the right place."

The office looks at first like it might be closed. But as we get closer, a dim light inside tells me there's someone inside. Thorn pulls open the rickety door and motions for me to go through.

Inside, an older, sort of doughy-looking woman is sitting behind an old, green metal desk. She looks like what I'd imagine Mrs. Santa Claus to look like — if Mrs. Santa Claus had badly-dyed red hair and wore loud polyester blend sweaters. Her face is round and apple-cheeked, and she's got on round wire-frame glasses that complete the effect. The woman looks up as the door opens, and gives me an automatic, efficient smile with bright pink lipsticked lips.

"Well, hello there!" she nods, first at me, then at Thorn. "How are you today?"

"We need a cottage," Thorn says without preamble.

"Of course!" The woman's smile fades for just a second, but then returns in force. "I'm assuming you don't have a reservation, since I have no record of anyone coming in today."

Thorn nods once. "That's right."

"All right, then." The woman reaches over to her right and opens a large appointment book of the kind I haven't seen in years. "You'll have your pick of places," she says as she reaches for a pen. "We don't get a lot of people here this time of year, seeing as it's off-season now. We usually have some visitors right after Christmas time every year, but that's about it until spring. Chester — that's my husband, Chester — keeps telling me we should close up shop in September, but I don't know. I think Lake Huron this time of year's something to be seen."

"It's our honeymoon," Thorn growls, interrupting her. "We want to be left *alone*."

I barely manage to suppress a snort.

The woman is a little startled, and takes a small step back. "Oh, certainly," she says hastily, reaching behind her to grab a key off a board on the wall. "Unit twenty-seven. It's the farthest cabin away from the main office. It's two miles up on the service road," she continues, pointing. "Far enough away from the other cabins, you can't even see your neighbors. 'Course, being as there aren't any other lodgers right now, you don't actually *have* any neighbors…"

"How much?" Thorn cuts her off.

Flustered, she tells him the cabin cost per night. Thorn reaches for his wallet and peels off a stack of bills. "Here. We'll take it for three weeks."

"Three *weeks*?" She repeats in disbelief. "At this time of year? Won't you be…"

Stepping forward, I take Thorn's arm and snuggle close to him. I look at the woman and do a simpering little giggle, then down at the ground like I'm embarrassed.

"Well," she concedes. I catch her glancing at my ringless hand.

"We got married pretty suddenly," I drawl. "Haven't had the chance to get the ring yet."

"Well…" she says again. She fingers the bills in her hand. "Three weeks it is, then," she says brightly. She hands Thorn the key.

"There's baseboard heaters, and a fireplace in each of the units." The woman begins to rattle off a list, in a tone that suggests she's done this a hundred times before. "Fully equipped kitchen, clean linens. The office is closed on Saturday and Sunday during the off season. Any problems, there's a laminated sheet hanging in the kitchen with the office phone number and my personal cell. There's a list of local businesses in the area as well. Maid service is —"

"No maid service," Thorn barks. "We'll come to you if we need anything. Thanks."

"Are you sure?" the woman asks, hesitating. "We can certainly accommodate —"

But Thorn has already grabbed my hand and is pulling me back outside. I look back and give the woman an apologetic wave as we leave.

"Thorn," I hiss in protest. "There was no reason to be so rude to her."

"Rude is good," he counters. "Rude tells her we don't want her hanging around asking more questions about us. Or getting it into her head to bake us fucking cookies or something. She seems like the type."

I want to continue arguing, but I have to concede that Thorn has a point there. Anyway, we're back at the SUV now, so I climb in silently and watch as Thorn puts the car in gear and drives in the direction of our new home for the next few weeks.

When we get to the cabin, both of us get to work unloading our bags and supplies. I put away the groceries. Thorn finds the thermostat, checks that the plumbing works, and gets to work building a fire with the wood stacked next to the fireplace. I make a quick dinner for us, as we're both hungry and exhausted from being in the car all day.

Thorn's mostly silent at dinner, though he answers me without any gruffness when I talk to him. I know he feels responsible for my safety, and I know he's preoccupied, so I try not to hold it against him. Our routine feels similar in some ways to what it was back at the safe house, but it's also completely different now that we're on the run. Now that we're safe, at least for the moment, I can't stop my thoughts from drifting back to what was happening between Thorn and me before he heard the would-be intruder lurking outside. It feels like the spell has been broken between us, and I can't help but mourn what we started last night, and wish I could get it back.

An involuntary shiver runs through me as I remember the feel of his lips against my skin, the rough stubble of his beard contrasting with the warm softness of his kiss. Thorn took me like a man possessed. As soon as he touched me, it was as if all the signals our bodies had been sending each other since the day we met finally exploded at once. Thinking about it now, I grow wet with need, and a wave of loneliness washes over me as I remember how good it felt when he held me in his arms after we both came together.

Suppressing a moan, I shift in my seat at the small table where we're eating dinner and steal a glance at Thorn. What I wouldn't give to have his mouth trace a path down my body again, to have his tongue plunge between my legs, teasing, tormenting me so deliciously…

"I've got to make a call," Thorn says abruptly, startling me. He pushes his chair roughly back from the table and stalks outside before I can respond.

Gloomily, I stand and take the dirty plates to the sink to wash them. I don't know if I've done something to upset him — though I wasn't even talking to him. Whatever it is, it looks like he's back to being gloomy, silent Thorn. Whatever happened between us last night at the safe house is no more than a fading memory, no matter how much I want it to happen again.

With a sigh, I clean up the dinner dishes and put everything away. Ten minutes later, I'm finished, and Thorn is still outside on the phone. Feeling aimless, I wander through the little cabin. It's smaller than the safe house was, but unlike the safe house, there are two bedrooms here, both of them tiny. The smaller of them holds two bunk beds stacked one on top of the other and nothing else. The slightly larger one has a single queen bed, and barely enough room for the low dresser which is the only other piece of furniture in the room. Thorn has tossed both of our bags on the bed in the larger room. For a moment, my heart leaps at the sight of them there. But then I realize he probably just threw them here for convenience, and that it doesn't mean anything.

I sit down on the bed, my shoulders slumping, and look aimlessly around. There are two pictures on the wall above the headboard. They're both views of the lake, one taken in summer and one in winter. The walls are painted a pale blue, a little scuffed here and there. It's homey, and tidy. Nothing glamorous, but a far cry from the motel where we spent last night.

Looking for something to do, I turn to my bag and decide to put my things away in the little dresser. As I reach into start taking things out, I'm wondering whether I should leave room for Thorn's things, or whether he'll be moving in next door. I glance over at his bag, and notice it's open, the flaps of the duffel parted to reveal some of its contents.

And that's when I glimpse something that makes me stop what I'm doing and stare.

The leather strap of a small purse.

My purse.

I haven't seen it since the night my father's men abducted me from the roadhouse. It never occurred to me that Thorn would still have it.

Which means he might also have my phone. My license. My credit cards. The pepper spray. It might all be in there.

I hardly even know what I'm doing as I start to reach for it. But just as my fingers make contact with the strap, a thump in the direction of the front door tells me that Thorn is back. I pull my hand back like I've been burned. Standing up quickly, my heart thudding, I make a beeline for the small bathroom and lock myself in before he comes in. I need a minute to compose myself and think.

22
THORN

After last night, being alone with Isabel is driving me fucking mad.

It was fine enough when we were on the run. I had a distraction. I was focused on getting her away from the safe house, and finding us another place to hide.

But now, we're back to where we were before, with one big difference.

Now, I know how good it feels to fuck her.

It feels like an eternity ago, last night. It's only been twenty-four hours.

Twenty-four hours since I've felt the heat of her, the softness of her. Twenty-four hours since she came all over my cock. Since I exploded on her stomach.

I feel like I'm jumping out of my skin as I shove away from the table after dinner. "I've got to make a call," I mutter, and get outside as fast as I can.

I don't have to make a call. I'm not due to ring Oz until tomorrow. And anyway, I don't have a lot to tell him, except that Isabel is safe.

I need to get away and think for a bit.

There's a small path leading away from the cottage toward the lake. I walk down to the shore and stare out at the water. I've never been to one of the Great Lakes before. It's a calm night, and the waves are larger than I expect. I look across the moonlit water. It's like an ocean, almost. I can't see the other side at all. The water crashes against the rocks and sand as it comes into shore.

I lost my head last night. I wasn't thinking.

I did exactly what I never should have let myself do.

I don't regret it.

And at the same time, I regret the hell out of it.

Fucking Isabel makes everything more complicated. It clouds my judgment regarding every decision I make from here on out about her. I can't afford to have feelings for someone I need to protect. I know that.

I can't afford to trust anyone but myself here.

The closer I get to Isabel, the more danger we run that I'll make a mistake.

"It can't happen again," I say out loud into the still night air.

But even as I say it, I know it's a lie.

I can try to stay away from Isabel. But I know it's too late. Every minute I try to resist her is just one more minute closer to the inevitable moment when I take her again.

When I get back in the house, Isabel's closed up in the bathroom. The dishes from dinner are put away. A wave of fatigue hits me, but I fight it off. I think about making some coffee.

Isabel comes out into the main room. She's dressed in a simple white T-shirt and jeans, her hair tied up loose, so that some strands of it fall around her face. She looks beautiful. So beautiful that it's almost hard to look at her, but even harder to look away.

"You look tired," she says, coming up to me.

I shrug off her concerned frown. "I'm fine," I reply. "Why don't you go to bed? I'll stay out in the living room."

"You're not going to try to stand guard all night again?" she asks in disbelief. "Thorn, you haven't slept in almost two days." When I don't answer, she tries again. "How can you protect me if you haven't had any sleep?" she points out. "You can't do this forever."

I see what she's doing. She's trying to appeal to my sense of reason.

"How can I trust you not to do anything stupid if I'm not awake to stop you?" I retort. I'm not really angry at her, but anger is the only shield I have against my mounting desire at having her so close.

"What could I possibly do out here?" she challenges, taking another step toward me.

"The office isn't far away. How do I know you won't make a run for it and go to them for help?"

Isabel lets out a breath and laughs softly. "I'm not about to go anywhere, Thorn," she says, her voice quiet. She looks up at me with those deep brown eyes. "I don't have anywhere to go. And I know I'm safest with you."

My cock tightens as I watch the pulse in her neck. It's fluttering like a hummingbird's. "That's exactly what someone who was planning to run would say," I rasp.

The air around us seems to still.

"Why don't you just tie me up then?" she says breathily. "So I don't try to escape?"

Her eyes are still locked on mine. I see her lids flutter. Her olive skin flushes. *Fuck*. She's baiting me. We're not talking about her running for it anymore.

She's pissing me off. I want to make her pay for what she's doing.

I want to make her *beg*.

I brought rope with me, throwing it into my bag mostly out of reflex just in case. But there's no time for that now. Before she can react, I reach down and lift Isabel in my arms, carrying her into the bedroom. I hear her breath catch in her throat, half-apprehensive, half turned on.

I throw her on the bed, and then I'm stradding her, my cock straining against my zipper. I grab her wrists with one hand and pull them over her head. With the other I undo my belt. I wrap it around her wrists, and roughly yank on it to tie it to the bedframe. All the while, Isabel keeps staring at me with a hungry challenge in her eyes. Her lips part. Her breasts rise and fall rapidly.

I stand up, undoing the button and zipper on my jeans. I take out my thick, stiff shaft and palm it.

"You're fucking maddening, you know that?" I growl at her hoarsely.

"I could say the same about you," she pants.

I begin to stroke myself, slowly, deliberately. Isabel's eyes are on me. She arches her back. Her hips thrust involuntarily.

"Thorn," she moans.

I know I'm fucking up again. But it's impossible to care.

Isabel is tied up and waiting for me, like the Christmas present I always wanted. She's all I can see, all I can smell, all I can feel.

I'm going to make her *beg*.

My dick throbs. A bead of precum shines at the head. Fuck, it's gonna be hard to take this slow at first.

Her jeans slip off easily. Isabel lifts her perfect ass and shimmies her hips to help me. Her T-shirt proves to be a problem, as her hands are bound, so I reach to the bottom of the shirt and rip it off her. She gasps, but keeps her eyes fixed on me as I pull the fabric away and toss it to the floor. I yank off my own T-shirt and kick my jeans to the floor before kneeling back down on the bed and straddling her again. My cock is pulsing, rising and falling just above her stomach. Isabel licks her lips, and I raise my hips up so she can take the head in her mouth.

Isabel's warm, wet lips envelop me. *Fucking Christ.* It's agony. It's perfect. Keeping her eyes on me, she swirls her tongue around the hot skin, licking and tasting. Her eyes flutter half-closed and she moans. I raise my hips a little more and she eagerly takes me deeper. I want to keep going like this, fuck her mouth until I explode down her throat. It takes everything I have to thrust slowly, controlling myself, until I feel my balls start to tighten and I have to back off. Pulling away, I stifle a groan, and slide myself back between her parted thighs.

"I'll teach you to challenge me," I growl thickly.

"Do your best," she gasps.

"Quiet," I command. "Or I'll be forced to shut that smart mouth up for you."

Her eyes flash, as though she's going to talk back, but I reach between her legs and slide a finger across her wet, waiting clit. She moans and throws her head back. Isabel arches her hips toward my touch, wanting more. I back away and she whimpers.

"What do you want, Isabel?" I rasp. Her only response is a low moan. "Tell me. I want to hear you say the words, Isabel."

"I…" she pants. "I want… you. I want more. What we did last night."

"What did we do last night?" I urge.

Isabel's face flames. "We… you fucked me. You made me come."

"That's what you want? You want me to make you come?"

Isabel squeezes her eyes shut. She nods frantically. "Yes," she whispers.

"Say it, then."

"I want you to fuck me, Thorn. Please, make me come."

My dick feels like it's going to explode. Watching that smart mouth beg me. Seeing her breasts heave with desire. I don't know how I'll ever be able to do without Isabel in my bed when this is all over. I've never wanted a woman the way I want her.

But for now, I do what I've learned to do, when faced with the unimaginable. I block it out.

For now, I take what's mine. And for now, what's mine is Isabel.

23
ISABEL

Having my hands tied above me is torture. I want to reach for Thorn, to touch him, to thread my hands in his hair as his mouth punishes mine with a hard, demanding kiss. My body is taut, tense like a rubber band with a need that I can't satisfy. I hear the moans ripping from my throat and I can't stop them. My back arches involuntarily as his head lowers toward me, holding my breath until his lips fasten around one taut nipple. I let out a soft cry as his mouth begins to tease and suck. I feel a rush of heat and wetness between my legs. I'm so ready for him to enter me, I can *feel* what it will be like after last night and I can hardly stand waiting for it. God, I want him to fill me, stretch me, take me. I want to watch his face, hard and tense as he thrusts into me. I want him to destroy me.

My body is trembling, every nerve ending craving his touch. His rough hands slide over my skin, gripping me, caressing me, *owning* me. All I can do is give myself up to him, and try not to go out of my mind with need. I hear myself whispering his name, and I know I'm begging but I can't stop. His mouth leaves my nipple, and then before I know it he's thrusting my knees wide and plunging his tongue inside my core, lapping at the wetness. I'm so close that I know it's only seconds before I'll come, but Thorns seems to know it too because he backs off almost instantly. I cry out in frustration, but in response all I hear is his low chuckle.

"You learning your lesson yet, Sibéal?" he rumbles thickly. Just hearing the raw lust in his voice makes me shiver.

"I don't know what you're talking about," I gasp.

"That right?" His head comes up. "You want to watch a film or something, then?"

"Thorn!" I cry out frantically, and he bursts out laughing.

"That's what I thought."

"You want it too," I whisper.

"Yes." His voice is instantly hard and hoarse. "Fuck if I don't want you more than is good for me. And for you." He leans down again, his hot breath teasing the sensitive skin of my thigh. "I'll make you pay for making me want you like this, Sibéal," he growls. "Are you ready to pay?"

"Yes." My voice cracks. Whatever he's about to do to me, I want it. I want it *desperately*.

Thorn's mouth closes over my swollen mound. A jolt of pleasure runs through me, and I spread my legs further and arch up to meet him. I'm so afraid he'll back away and torture me, but instead his tongue begins to taste and tease. It's a delicious agony, so good it's almost unbearable. Sparks feel like they are shooting from my entire body as he licks me. I writhe against the belt binding my wrists. Again I hear myself start to mumble incoherent things, my breathing growing fast and shallow, waiting as desire starts to rise like a tidal wave in me. "Thorn!" I gasp, as it builds and I start to lose control. Then all at once, I fly off the edge, shattering as the wave crashes over me, over and over again.

Thorn kneels between my legs as my orgasm continues to shake me, and slides himself inside me. Being filled by him just makes the pleasure more intense, and I continue to come around him as he throws my legs over his shoulders and begins to thrust hard and deep. His fingers grip hard into my thighs as he pulls me against him. Inside, the head of his cock presses against something I've never felt before, something that makes me *need* release even though I just came. Thorn must feel it, too, because his eyes meet mine and he rolls his hips with every thrust, hitting that spot over and over again as I cry out and throw my head back.

"Don't pull out," I whisper as I climb higher and higher. "When you come, don't pull out."

"I don't have any condoms," he warns me.

"I'm on the shot." I've never been more grateful for it than I am right now. I *need* Thorn inside me, more than anything.

As I surrender to the tidal wave one more time, I feel my muscles clench around his shaft. Thorn tenses, his cock growing larger inside me. Finally, he rocks hard against me one more time.

"Isabel!" he roars. He comes so hard I can feel his liquid heat as he empties himself inside me. I close my eyes, arching my neck back at how good it feels to be filled up by him like this. I feel whole. Complete.

At some point, while I'm still in the throes of pleasure, Thorn unties my wrists. He pulls me to him, cradling me in his powerful arms as he takes me into the bed next to him. He pulls the covers up over us. I wrap my arms around him tightly and try to still my breathing and my hammering heart, as though I'm clinging onto him for dear life. When my breath finally calms, I slip into the deepest sleep I've had in months.

* * *

We end up staying at the cabin for more than a week.

I know in theory we're still in danger. And I know I should hate being here, isolated and in hiding. But I don't. Not at all.

Unlike the boredom I felt at the safe house, being here — with Thorn — starts to feel almost like a vacation to me. Sometimes I even find myself forgetting the reason we're here in the first place.

During the day, we watch movies, make love, talk, eat. Thorn is still watchful, and even tense at times. But he seems to have started to believe I'm not going anywhere. Sometimes he goes outside to make a call, or brood, or think. He doesn't tell me who he's calling, or what's being said, and I don't ask. I occupy myself during his absences by reading my borrowed Kindle. Every leading man in every romance novel I read becomes Thorn. Every sex scene I read makes me seek him out to satisfy the ache between my legs. I find little ways to tease him, seduce him subtly and not so subtly, making it seem like I'm not doing it on purpose. I wear the skimpiest clothes I can find, and then ask Thorn to build up the fire until it's so hot inside the cabin that I have to take even more things off. Or I take a shower, and come out of the bathroom with a tiny towel wrapped around me and wander around until he grabs me and pulls it off.

I can't remember being happier in my life. It's almost like we're really on a honeymoon, like Thorn told the woman at the resort office we were.

We're here so long that eventually, Thanksgiving comes. Thorn surprises me by going into town one morning while I'm still sleeping and getting a chicken to roast. "Sorry, we'll have to pretend it's a turkey," he says with a twinkle in his eye when he comes back with the groceries. "And I got some of that cranberry sauce shite in a can."

I laugh. "Actually, I love that stuff. I don't know what it is about the canned version, but I like it better than actual cranberries."

"So, actual cranberries are real?" he asks dubiously. "I thought they were just a fake thing. Like circus peanuts."

"Oh, circus peanuts," I croon. "I like those, too."

"What in the fuck is wrong with you, woman?" Thorn looks seriously offended. "Those are the Devil's sweets."

"Don't hate," I shoot back.

"I'm not hating," he frowns. "I just think you might be needing your head examined."

I'm feeling happy and festive as I cobble together a sort of Thanksgiving dinner from what we have on hand. Thorn, of course, doesn't really care about the holiday. I'm touched that he even remembered it, much less thought to let me celebrate it. I spend the day cooking as he sits on the couch and tries to find something to watch on TV. We watch part of the Macy's parade, which he thinks is stupid, and I argue with him just because it's fun.

When the food is ready, we sit down at the tiny kitchen table and eat. Thorn opens a bottle of beer for each of us. I've overdone the chicken a little, and the mashed potatoes are from a bag. But even so, strangely, this is the most fun I can remember having at Thanksgiving since I was a kid. Even Thorn seems to be feeling it a little, as he loosens up and consents to talking about himself more than I've been able to get him to since I met him.

"You don't celebrate Thanksgiving in Ireland, right? Obviously," I ask, lifting a forkful of chicken to my mouth.

"No. 'Course not." He smirks at me in amusement, and I resist the urge to feel dumb for asking the question.

"You must have done Thanksgiving before, though, since you've been living in the States?"

"Once or twice." He shrugs. "Mostly, I just leave the day to you lot."

I'm quiet for a second. I want to know more, but I'm afraid he'll be angry if I push.

"Do you miss the holidays in Ireland?" I finally ask. "Christmas?"

Thorn blinks. "Sort of," he shrugs, and leans back in his chair. "It's been a long time now. I don't think about it much."

"It must be... a little strange spending it here," I venture. "Without your family."

"My family was sort of rubbish." He snorts softly. "Except for Jimmy."

Something in the way his voice goes flat catches my attention. Thorn's staring ahead, into space, and I can see he's momentarily lost in thought. My gut twists; suddenly, I'm *sure* there's a story behind his words. A story that will tell me more about Thorn than almost anything else.

I want him to keep talking, but I'm terrified one wrong word will slam the door shut.

"Who's Jimmy?" I finally say, holding my breath.

Thorn glances over at me, almost as though he's surprised there's someone else there. "Oh, Jimmy," he says in an offhand tone. "He was me cousin."

Was.

"I grew up with him. Lived in the same house with him. His ma was my ma's sister."

"Were you the same age?"

"Eh? Oh, no. He was seven years younger." The ghost of a smile plays on Thorn's lips. "He was sort of a younger version of meself, though. The two of us had mothers who didn't amount to much. Mine was a boozer. My da' was long gone. Jimmy's ma came to live with us when Jimmy was born. She was a piece of work, that one." His mouth curls in disgust. "She whored around, always lookin' for a man to take care of her. But all she did was bring her mess back to the house, for the rest of us to deal with."

Thorn's slight accent thickens just a bit as he talks. I don't interrupt, waiting for him to go on.

"Our mas were gone a fair amount. So it fell to me to take care of Jimmy. I didn't mind it. He was a good little lad. He looked up to me. Imagine that." Thorn snickers, but the sound has a sad ring to it. He sighs. "My aunt would bring this endless string of scumbags around, each of them worse than the last. Eventually, she brought 'round the worst of the lot." He sneers. "Eamon Bernagh."

Thorn turns to me. "I was born in a place called Finglas. I don't imagine you've heard of it." When I shake my head, he continues. "It's part of Dublin. A part known for stabbings and shootings. And all manner of criminal activity. Eamon Bernagh was a petty thug with delusions of grandeur. Somehow, my aunt Yvonne fell in with him. Well, he brought all his shite along with him, didn't he? He ran afoul of the wrong people, trying to take too big a piece of the pie for himself.

"One day, Eamon came to our place asking for Yvonne to hide him. She said yes, even though she knew my ma would never have allowed it. We didn't know anything about it until later. All we knew was that suddenly, Eamon was hanging around all the time. This was one of the rare times that both my ma and Yvonne were working, so I was responsible for making sure Jimmy got home from school, did his schoolwork, didn't open the door to strangers and whatnot. 'Course, I was sixteen years old. Babysitting my cousin wasn't my idea of a good time." The slight smile he gives me is tinged with regret. "Bit of a delinquent, even then.

"One day I left the apartment to talk to a girl I was interested in who lived in our block." Thorns eyes grow somber, distant. "When I came back, the door was open and I could hear noises inside. There were two men, toward the back of the house, and they had Jimmy. I knew who they must be looking for.

"We had a gun in the house, because of Eamon. In the drawer of Yvonne's nightstand. I knew more about guns at that age than I ought. I knew how to use it." Thorn grimaces. "Trouble was, I couldn't get a clear shot. The thug trying to scare Jimmy into telling him where Eamon was had a gun to his head."

Thorn takes a deep breath in, and when he lets it out, there's a dead weight to his voice I've never heard before. "I was afraid I'd shoot Jimmy instead of him." Thorn's voice cracks as he says these words. He clears his throat, looking down and shaking his head, sorrow etched in his features. When he looks back up at me, his eyes are filled with pain. "He was just a kid. I loved the little bugger," he rasps. "But that was just the problem. I hesitated just a second too long." He clears his throat again. "The thug looked up, saw me, and pulled the trigger. Not sure he meant to, but he blew Jimmy's head off all the same. I took aim and shot him. Then I shot the other man who came in from looking through the house trying to find whatever it was Eamon had that they wanted."

"Thorn," I whisper, my hand covering my mouth. "Oh my God."

"The first fucker died," he continues tiredly, almost as if I hadn't spoken. "The second one lived, long enough to tell his boss who shot him, at least. They got Eamon the next day." Thorn stands up and goes to a cupboard. He opens it and takes out a bottle of amber-colored liquid, then a shot glass. "I ran for it. Hid out at a friend's house for a couple of days. My ma was able to scrape together some money for a plane ticket." He pours himself a shot, and downs it. "She sent me to live with an uncle in America."

"That's why you haven't been back," I murmur. Suddenly, I feel cold.

"There's still a price on my head. There's no going back." Thorn shakes his head and pours another shot. "And anyway, I wouldn't want to be there. Memories of Jimmy would be everywhere. Seein' all the things he'd never get to grow up to do. And knowin' it's my fault."

"Thorn…" I begin, but stop. I want to say it's not his fault, because it isn't. Of course it isn't. But I know instinctively that he doesn't want to hear it. I watch as he downs another shot and immediately spills out a third one.

"So," he concludes grimly. "I left Ireland. I came to the States. Got work with me uncle. Eventually, I fell in with the Lords." He looks at me with a wry, tight half-smile. "And now I'm here."

I hold his gaze. "Thank you for telling me that, Thorn," I murmur. "I'm so sorry."

He nods, but looks away, his mind already elsewhere. "I'm going to go get some air," he announces, standing up.

He takes the bottle with him.

I watch him walk out the door into the night. The spell between us is broken. I don't try to follow him. As much as I want to heal the hurt that clearly still burns inside him, I know I can't. I know he needs to be alone right now.

I get up and put the food away. I wash the dishes. An hour later, he's still not back.

My heart feels like it's cracking in half. I get ready for bed, look miserably out the window into the dark, and finally slip under the cold covers, hoping that Thorn will come help me warm them in the night.

24
ISABEL

Thorn comes back inside sometime after I've fallen asleep. When I wake up the next morning, he's not in bed. I pull on some clothes and pad out into the main room. He's up already, making coffee in the kitchen. On the couch is a thick afghan and a pillow.

He's distant all that day, barely talking to me unless I say something to him or ask him a question. And even then, he seems to come out of a fog, turning to blink at me as though he's forgotten I'm there.

As the day wears on, he goes from simply silent to almost radiating tension. When the sun goes down, he pulls down the whiskey bottle and pours himself a few shots. Then he switches to beer.

That night, as I'm getting ready for bed, he comes into the bedroom and startles me from behind. His mouth comes down on mine, rough and demanding. He takes me silently, almost savagely, and it's wanton and hard, and I want it so badly I almost cry that he's come to me at last. Afterward, he climbs into bed with me and doesn't say a word. He falls asleep almost instantly.

The next morning, he's a little better — a little more cheerful — but it doesn't last long. As the day wears on he grows more brooding again. He spends long stretches outside, standing guard in front of the little cabin like a watchdog. That night, he comes back in again, and we eat dinner in silence. And when it's time to go to bed, he comes in with me, and takes me again, hard, fast, and frantic, like it's our last night on earth.

I know — or rather, I sense — that the story Thorn told me about his family, and about his cousin Jimmy, is what's eating at him. But I don't know how to help him. And every time I try to bring up the subject, the words die in my throat. Because when he looks at me at those moments, his eyes are dark with warning, and impossibly far away. Every moment of intimacy we've shared seems lost then.

I try to tell myself I should just be content with what I have. The sex is almost frighteningly good, after all. Even when Thorn looks at me like a man possessed. Even when he rolls away from me afterward, or when he holds me so close and so tightly I almost can't breathe.

He's just my guard, after all. Or my captor. Or my protector. I don't know what he is anymore. Is this Stockholm Syndrome I'm feeling? Or something else?

The truth is, I do know. I just don't want to admit it. Not to myself, and definitely not to him.

I spent a good part of my childhood and most of my adolescence watching my mother try to make it work with an MC president. I have early memories of my dad living with us. Except for the most part, those memories are of a large, dark man smelling of leather and smoke, his voice deep and kind of frightening for a little girl. I remember the arguments they used to have. I remember one year, when I was four or five, listening through the closed door of my bedroom as my mother yelled at him for not being there for my birthday celebration. She was angrier than I had ever heard her be. The funny thing was, it never occurred to me that the big mountain of the man I knew as Daddy would be there to watch me blow out the candles or open my presents. He was someone who lived with us sometimes. Nothing more.

My parents finally split up for good when I was ten. Though my mom would never bad-mouth my father in front of me, I know she was sick of him considering his old lady and daughter as a distant afterthought in his life. Listening to her try crying quietly in her bedroom at night so I wouldn't hear — watching her try to make it work as a single mom — taught me the lesson that men like my father couldn't be trusted. They were too far inside themselves. They didn't know how to love. It was folly to hope for more than they could give you.

My mother loved Oz, I know. Hell, maybe she still loves him. All these years later, she's never brought another boyfriend home. She's lived like a nun, being a mother and caretaker to me. And now, being a caregiver to her parents in Venezuela. As much as I love her, the path of her life has always read like a cautionary tale to me. I told myself I'd never be with a man like Oz. The heartache wasn't worth it.

And now here I am.

The truth is, I'm pretty sure I've fallen in love with him. I don't even know how it happened.

And I'm just realizing it right at the moment when he's pulling away.

I don't know how to keep him. I don't know how to stop the way I feel. Worst of all, I know that every night, when he comes to me, I won't push him away. I want him too much. I'm afraid that by the end of this I'll be half-crazy, and ruined for other men. Because as young as I am, I already know there could never be anyone else for me like Thorn.

God. I must be the stupidest person on the planet.

During those days when Thorn is so distant, I find my mind going back frequently to the image of my purse strap peeking out of his bag the first day we got here. I'm lonely here now that he's barely talking to me. And I keep wondering whether my cell phone is in my purse. And my pepper spray, and my license and credit cards and all the rest.

My tickets to the outside world.

Two weeks ago, I would have grabbed that purse and run like hell. I still could, I know. I have shoes now. And like Thorn said, if I could make it down to the main office, I'm sure I could beg them to help me find a way out of here. But now, the idea dies in my mind almost as soon as I have it. I know down deep that Thorn is the only one who can protect me. I know I'm safer with him than I would be anywhere else.

And worst of all, I don't want to leave him. I want to stay here, next to him. I want the Thorn I saw the first week we were here at the cabin. Before he told me about Jimmy, and closed himself off from me.

With *that* Thorn here with me, I might not ever want to leave.

But as it is, I'm getting homesick. And my loneliness gets worse every day without Thorn to talk to. I'm desperate for a friendly voice. Just for a little bit. Just to remind me that there's still a world out there, and that I had a place in it. And that someday, maybe I'll be able to go back to it.

One afternoon, Thorn is sitting at the small table cleaning the gun he always carries, with tools from a small pouch that he must have brought with him. I'm actually jealous that he has something to occupy him. I'm sitting on the couch, flipping through the few channels we get on the small TV, with my Kindle by my side. By now I've read the everything in the entire library, some books more than once. Hell, I've even read through a cookbook about Vietnamese food that's on there. And I don't even like Vietnamese food.

I'm trying to decide whether to re-read one of the books when an idea hits me.

"Thorn, could we maybe take a trip into the nearest town?" I ask, in what I hope is not too much of a pleading tone. "Get some playing cards or magazines or something, to pass the time? I could buy some boo—"

"No."

I suppress a sigh and try again. "We're going to start to run out of food soon…"

"I'm aware of that," he bites out, jaw tense.

"So, maybe we should go stock up on groceries?"

"No," he repeats. A muscle in his jaw twitches.

"Well, what are we —"

"*Isabel!*" he shouts, making me jump. "Will you just shut up and let me handle it!"

"Then *handle* it!" I yell back. "I'm turning in circles around this place! I feel like I'm going crazy! It's a special kind of torture to make me just stay here with nothing to do but wander around the cabin and look out the window!"

"Maybe I should tie you back up then," he snarls, rounding on me. "Then you won't have the decision to make whether you should walk in circles in the bedroom, or the living room, or the kitchen. How would that be?"

"Why are you *being* this way?" I cry. "It's not my fault we're here! None of this is my fault! It's not my fault I was born to a man who makes enemies easier than he breathes! I don't *want* to be in the middle of all this any more than you do! You act like I'm personally responsible for making you do this job!"

"Jesus Christ, woman, I know that!" Thorn runs an angry hand through his dark hair. "But you're sure as hell not making it any easier! You seem to think this is a little vacation honey—" He stops short. "We're not here to have *fun*, Isabel. I'm here to make sure you're not killed!"

"How the hell can I be killed if no one has any idea where we are!" I roll my eyes. "My dad doesn't know, his men don't know… Your *club* doesn't even know!"

"Yes, and I'm gonna fuckin' keep it that way," he grits. "And not by taking you into town to go *antiquing* or some shite!"

"When the hell did I say I wanted to go *antiquing*! I said I wanted to go get some groceries before we run out of food and starve to death!" Thorn snorts, but I keep going. "And yeah, I was hoping maybe we could get some books or something to occupy our time! So I'm bored! So I'm human! Sue me! God, aren't you bored, too?"

"Fuck yes, I'm bored! Jesus! But too fucking bad! This is my job! Whether I'm bored or not is irrelevant. That's what being in an MC is!" He throws his hands out impatiently. "You do whatever is necessary, whatever your president tells you to do. Because it's your duty. Even if your duty is complete bollocks, like playing bodyguard for some spoiled little MC princess!"

I recoil like he's slapped me. I can't believe after all of this, he thinks I'm spoiled. I can't believe that after everything we've been through together — everything we've done together — he just thinks of me as some pathetic little girl.

"You know what, Thorn? *Forget* it!" I cry, stomping toward the bedroom. I spin on my heel and look at him with all the venom I can muster. "You are a fucking asshole, Thorn!" I hiss. "A fucking *asshole!*"

I slam the door behind me before he can reply and flop down on the bed, my chin trembling. I'm bewildered and upset that things between us got out of control so quickly. I already feel a little bad about it. I know Thorn is probably just as bored as I am. And I know he's doing his best. But it's driving me crazy that he won't talk to me. And I guess I just wanted to goad him into saying *something*. But now we're fighting. And even though I am just a little sorry, I'm more angry at him, and I'll be damned if I apologize first.

A few seconds later, I hear a loud thump, and then the ever-familiar sound of Thorn leaving the house. I squeeze my eyes shut, let out a wail of despair, and try not to start crying.

After all, crying is exactly what a spoiled little MC princess *would do,* I think bitterly. *Fuck him. Fuck everything about him!*

As much as I try to push them down, a few tears make their way to the surface and roll down my cheeks. Angrily, I brush them away. *Well, here I am again. All alone.* And things are likely to be even worse between us when he gets back. Even more silent and tense, as if that's even possible.

I stand and go to the bedroom door. Opening it, I go to the kitchen and get myself a glass of water, which I drink standing over the sink. I make my rounds wandering about the cabin, looking at things I've already looked at a hundred times. Kitchen. Living room. Unused second bedroom. Bathroom. The bedroom I've started thinking of as "our" room.

Ha.

I'm contemplating whether maybe I should just try to take a nap, when something catches my attention out of the corner of my eye. Turning, I notice Thorn's duffel bag. Normally, it's lying closed on a chair in the corner of the room, but right now it's unzipped and sitting on the dresser. He must have opened it to take out the kit to clean his gun.

It's right there. Not three feet away from me.

I could reach inside right now. Just to see if the purse is still there.

Ignoring the warning bells clanging inside me, I step toward the bag and put my hand in. Blindly, I fish around, and in a couple of seconds my fingers brush against a familiar strap. Guilt makes my stomach flip unpleasantly, but I tell myself I don't care.

I pull up on the strap. The purse emerges from his bag like a fish on a line.

My God. It's been so long since I've seen it, it feels almost unreal to be holding it again. A symbol of my life *before* all this. When I had no idea why my father was being so ridiculous, hiding me away like Rapunzel in a tower.

Before I ever met Thorn.

My hands shake a little as I unzip the main compartment and reach inside. I pull out my keys and set them beside Thorn's bag on the dresser. Then my pepper spray. Then a tube of lip gloss. Then my little wallet with my money, credit cards and ID.

Finally, my hands close over the cell phone and lift it out.

I stare at the thing in wonder, like it's a missive from another dimension. The screen is cracked just a little, and I remember it dropping to the ground when Oz's men grabbed me. The phone is off, and for one terrifying moment, I think the battery's dead. But when I hold down on the power switch, after a second the familiar light of the screen comes on, and I actually start *laughing*, I'm so excited.

I have to wait almost a full minute before the phone is totally powered up. Dozens of text messages and voicemails appear, most of them from Deb. I can only imagine how frantic she must have been, and how worried she probably is.

The phone doesn't have a lot of battery left, and I only have two bars of service. But it works.

Maybe…

Maybe I could call Deb. Just to tell her I'm alive, and I'm okay. To let her know I didn't mean to just disappear on her that night at Buzzy's.

Just to hear a friendly voice.

I'm already smiling in anticipation of having a little connection with the outside world as I find Deb in my contacts and press the call button. Holding the phone to my ear, it's actually comforting to listen to the familiar, *normal* ring.

"Hello? *Izzy?*" Deb's voice answers. I feel an almost dizzying rush of adrenaline.

I'm opening my mouth to answer when a roar of anger behind me makes me drop my phone.

"What the *fuck* are you doing?"

DAPHNE LOVELING

25
THORN

"What the *fuck* are you doing?" My voice booms through the room, startling Isabel so much she drops her mobile. I don't fucking care. My fists clench tight, and if they were around her neck right now they'd be itching to strangle her.

I cross the room in two steps and the thing is my hand before she can do anything to stop me. "I —" she starts to babble. "I wasn't doing —"

"*Don't* fucking *lie* to me, Isabel!" I shout. I glance down at the screen to see the fucking phone is *connected* to whatever number she's rung. The contact name says *Deb*. I hear a thin, tinny female voice screech through the receiver. "Hello? Izzy? Oh my God, is that you?"

I start to hold down the button to shut the damn thing off, but as soon as the screen goes black I let loose a roar of outrage and fling the fucking thing across the room. It crashes against the wall and falls to the floor. Isabel gapes at me, a mixture of fear and horror on her face. She backs away a few paces, putting the bed between her and me.

"What the fuck were you thinking!" I shout, closing the space between us until I'm towering over her. "After all of this, after *everything* that's happened, you're still trying to fucking *escape*?" My mind has gone numb from fury. I came in here from outside to try to make amends after yelling at her earlier. But instead, I find *this*. I glance over at my duffel, suddenly realizing she must have been digging through it. Sitting next to it on the dresser is her little purse and its contents, including a tube of pepper spray. Christ, was she planning on using *that* on me? My fists clench even tighter. Letting out another roar of anger, I turn and punch the wall, *hard*, so I don't hurt her instead. The pain is welcome. It focuses me, gives the anger somewhere to go.

"Thorn!" Isabel's voice cracks, barely above a whisper. I turn back to her, and my face must be something to see, because she shrinks away from me in horror and starts to tremble. "I swear," she whispers, shaking her head. "I swear, I wasn't trying to do what you think I was! I swear, I was only trying to make a quick call to my friend! The one I was with when Oz's men took me!" Her eyes fill. "I just wanted to hear a friendly voice, and tell her I'm okay!"

"You expect me to believe that?" I laugh incredulously. "Jesus fucking Christ!" I rake my hand through my hair.

"Yes! I do, because it's true!" she cries. Tears start to spill down her cheeks. "I promise Thorn! I swear, I wouldn't lie to you!"

"You wouldn't *lie* to me?!" I repeat, stunned. "What the fuck do you call this, then?" I sweep my hand toward the contents of her purse. Isabel at least has the sense to look ashamed. Her cheeks redden as she casts her eyes down toward the floor.

"I didn't mean to!" she insists, but her voice is unsteady, like she knows she's fighting a losing battle. "I just… I saw the strap of my purse in your bag a couple days ago and, well…" She looks up at me helplessly. "I'm sorry, Thorn… I'm just so lonely, and you're so angry at me all the time, and…" More tears slide down her cheeks. "I promise," she finishes in a desolate whisper. "I just wanted to talk to my friend for a couple of minutes. That's all."

Her lips are trembling as the tears continue to come. She makes little snuffling noises as she cries but tries to suppress them, staring down at the floor like she knows there's nothing more to say.

I shouldn't fucking believe her. I should assume every single bloody thing out of this girl's mouth is a lie. But in spite of myself, I do. It rings true, what she's saying. I've been staying away from her since the night I told her about Jimmy. At least during the day. It's for her own good, and our safety, to be sure. But at night, I haven't been able to stop myself from taking her. From coming back for more. She's like a drug.

I can see why she'd think I was angry at her. Even though I don't want to see it. I find myself trying to imagine what the last few days have been like for her. No one to talk to, nothing to do, and me leaving her alone inside to twiddle her thumbs while I stay outside and try to talk myself out of going to her bed again when the darkness comes.

Maybe it's only natural that eventually she'd look for some way to connect with a friend. Maybe it really is as simple as that.

I feel my anger draining out of me as quickly as it came. Most of it, anyway. There's still a bit left, because the fact is what she did was fucking stupid. And I tell her so, as I sit tiredly on the bed and rest my head in my hands.

"I just wanted to talk to Deb for a minute," Isabel says weakly, and leans against the wall. "She hasn't heard from me since the night I disappeared. She must be worried sick. I just wanted to tell her I was okay."

"Don't you realize the men who're looking for you could have traced the call?" I sigh. "Jesus, what an idiotic thing to do, Isabel."

"Don't call me an idiot!" she protests, a thin flare of her own anger coming to the surface.

"I didn't call you an idiot!" I bark back at her. "Besides, if you don't want me to call you an idiot, then stop acting like one!"

"Well, maybe you could just *talk* to me once in a while, then!" She throws up her hands in frustration. "God, Thorn, what do you expect me to do? I sit in this house all day by myself while you go out and do whatever. I don't even know what I've done to make you hate me so much all of a sudden!"

"Hate you?" Jesus, does she really not know?

"Yes!" She stomps her foot, then looks sort of ashamed that she's done something so childish. "It's not my fault, Thorn! I'm sorry my dad hired you — or forced you — to do this. I'm sorry I'm his daughter. I'm sorry I'm even here, messed up in all this! All I wanted was to just take my stupid classes at the stupid community college, and live my stupid life, far from the Death Devils and everything they represent. I didn't ask you to be here, and I wish to God I could just tell you to leave!"

"You do?"

My eyes meet hers, and she looks quickly away.

"I mean…" She trails off. "I just mean, I wish you didn't have to be messed up in all this."

"Isabel." I take a step toward her, trying to ignore the sudden stiffness of my cock as I notice how hard her nipples are under her shirt. "My job is to keep you safe. You are not helping me do that job by going behind my back."

"I know." Her voice is subdued. I hear just a trace of the breathiness in her throat that's there right before I plunge myself inside her. My shaft begins to throb.

"I swear to you," I say, grabbing her face in my hand and turning it toward me. "If you have any thoughts of trying to escape, don't. You won't live through it." I don't mean what *I'll* do to her. The thought of her in Fowler's hands creates a knot of nausea in the pit of my stomach. I see her as *he* would see her.

And I *know* what he would do to her before he killed her.

"I promise I didn't. I *don't*."

Isabel's voice is breathless. Her dark, stormy eyes are wide, frightened as she looks up at me. For the millionth time, my brain curses that I'm stuck protecting someone I don't want the responsibility for. Protecting a brother, that's one thing. Every man in the Lords of Carnage would die to protect the others. It's a vow we all made when we were patched in. We're all equals. We all signed on for the same thing. We have each other's backs. But *this*…

This… has *changed*.

My gut clenches as my brain wrestles with a thought that's forced its way in without my even knowing it.

This *used* to be about protecting a spoiled MC princess. It used to be a fucked-up job that I was doing because my club prez demanded it. And because the Lords needed it. I didn't give a damn about Oz, or the Death Devils, or this girl, beyond what it meant for the brothers I promised to ride and die for.

It used to be something I couldn't wait to be done with. So I'd never have to see Isabel again. Or so I told myself.

Here in the States, the life I left behind in Ireland is far away from me. Here, I don't have a mother, a family, a past. All I have is the club, and my role in it.

But as I stare down into Isabel's eyes — frightened but trusting — it's like she's a siren, calling me toward something I want to resist with everything I have in me.

"Thorn," she whispers. "Please forgive me. I didn't mean…" Her breath hitches. "I didn't mean to betray you. I just didn't think. All I wanted was to talk to someone who missed me." She blinks and looks away. "Just to remind myself I'm still… *real*. That I still exist, to the world outside."

My heart twists in sympathy for her. I know she didn't ask for this. But I make one more desperate attempt to push her away. "Jesus Christ, woman!" I say gruffly, frowning down at her instead. "What the fuck does that mean?"

"Stop that!" Isabel cries. She yanks herself out of my grasp and, rounds on me. "Stop calling me *woman* like it's an insult! Just because I don't have a… *cock*, doesn't mean you get to treat me like I'm some sort of idiot!"

Watching her plump lips as she stumbles over the word sends a jolt through my dick like she's just told me she wants to suck it. In spite of the tension between us, I have to laugh. "You don't like saying it," I growl at her. "But you sure do like it, don't you, girl?"

"Why do you get off on making me feel like shit?" she yells, flinging out her arms in exasperation. "Why do you hate me so much? What have I ever done to you?"

My body has a mind of its own as I grab her by the wrists and pull her to me. "I've told you already, I don't hate you," I growl against her ear. "That's the whole problem, Isabel. I've been trying to hate you since the day I met you. It's my bad luck I can't seem to manage it."

Isabel shivers and instinctively molds her body against mine, letting out a soft moan. Without even reaching between her legs to touch her, I know she's wet for me. Ready.

I can't hold back anymore. I've been fooling myself these last few weeks, telling myself the reason I can't stay away from her is just because she's here, she's close, and there's no one else around. But this is more than that. Much more. This girl's found her way inside me. At this point, even if her father told her my job was done, I'd protect and defend Isabel until my dying breath. It's no longer just a job to me. It's personal.

She belongs to me. Her body, her soul. Every orgasm she'll ever have. All of it: *Mine.*

It's time to show her that.

And then, it's time to end the motherfuckers who are trying to hurt her. Once and for all.

26
THORN

"I want to hate you," I rasp as I move between her legs. My cock is hard as a bat. "Don't you see, Isabel, it's better for you if I do."

Her naked thighs are trembling. I push them apart and plunge my tongue inside her. She gasps and arches toward me.

"But I'll be fucked if I can stay away from you. Hard as I try." Jesus, she tastes sweet as she writhes on my tongue. Her clit is hard, pulsing. She's soaking wet. Her hips thrust upward, needing my mouth on her, and I devour her, kissing, caressing, licking, as she moans and thrashes on the bed. I slip two fingers inside her, stroking and caressing until I find the spot that drives her wild. She tenses and cries out.

"You're mine, Isabel," I growl. My hot breath teases the sensitive flesh of her inner thigh and she shudders. She's already so close, and I can hardly wait to fuck her. My cock's so hard it hurts. If I don't get inside her soon, I'm going to shoot my load in my pants like a fucking teenager.

"Tell me you're mine," I insist.

She moans and clutches at the sheets. "I'm yours," she pants. "Oh, God, Thorn, please, I'm so close…"

"All of you. Your body is mine. Your pussy is mine. Everything. *Mine*."

"Yes…" she whispers, and then, all at once, her whole body freezes. A second later, she shatters, her orgasm ripping through her like wildfire. She keeps coming as I pull her toward me. I flip her over on her back, onto her knees, and bury myself deep inside her, up to the hilt. Jesus, she's so hot, so wet… I know exactly how it's going to feel now when I push inside her, but it's still a shock that it's always better than I think it's going to be. Isabel's head is pressed against the pillow but she pushes her hips back and meets me thrust for thrust, urging me deeper, her channel clutching my dick. I speed up, because I can't wait, I need to come inside her. One of my hands grabs her hip, hard and bruising, the other wraps her long hair around my fist. She's whimpering, but then the whimpers change to loud cries of pleasure and I know she's about to come again. "Come for me, baby," I croon as I feel my balls start to tighten.

"Thorn, I'm coming…" she mewls. Her channel contracts, and that's all it takes to send me over the edge. I thrust once more and explode, *claiming* her, coming so hard and so long I fill her up to the hilt with everything I've got.

Jesus Christ, it feels better than anything I've ever felt in my life.

I stay inside her, wrapping an arm around her and pulling her into the curve of me as I fall down onto the bed. We're both panting, breathing in rhythm, and it feels like even our heartbeats are in sync with one another. I can't talk, don't want to say what's on the tip of my tongue, because it's shit I've never said to any woman. It's shit you can't take back once you've said it.

Isabel's mine. I've told her that.

But I'm not prepared to tell her the rest.

That I'm hers, as well.

* * *

The next day, I've had enough of fucking waiting around. I ring Oz for an update. For once, he actually has something to tell me.

"I've been waiting for your call," he mutters into the phone. "I think I've figured out who the mole is in my organization. A traitorous snake named Playboy." Oz's voice instantly transforms to the cold-as-ice tone I've heard him use once or twice. It's a voice that should strike fear into the heart of any man it's directed toward. "I'm going to torture it out of him. And then, I'm going to kill him."

"If the guy I ended at our safe house is any indication, you won't get much." This Playboy must be a fuckin' idiot if he's put himself between two men as dangerous as Oz and Fowler. Either way, he's gonna be toast when one or the other finds out his cover is blown. I'd almost feel sorry for the guy, except he deserves everything that's coming to him.

I'm about to respond to Oz when suddenly, I get an idea.

"How sure are you he's the one feeding intel to Fowler?" I ask him.

"Almost positive."

"And he doesn't know that you know."

"Not yet." I hear his lip curl in disgust.

"Hold off, Oz. I have a better idea."

I tell him it's time to push this thing to its logical conclusion. "It's time to stop playing defense and go on the offense. To end Fowler and his organization, and take care of this threat once and for all."

And what I have in mind starts with the mole.

"Start talking to your club about the situation with Isabel, when the mole is there and can hear you," I say. "Tell them I've betrayed you. That I've abandoned Isabel. Say that she's called you, and that she's terrified and all alone in a cabin in Michigan. She's begging you to come get her. Tell them you're looking for someone to come up here, get her and bring her back home to you."

"The mole."

"Exactly. Make sure you stress that Isabel is alone. Isolated. That she has no defense."

Oz is silent for a moment. Then: "You think Fowler will come after her himself."

"Yes. I do," I affirm. "He's been waiting for weeks to get his hands on her. Knowing she's completely alone and there for the taking is likely to be just the lure he needs. It's the best way to get him out in the open. Maybe the only way."

"I will send my entire club." Oz's voice is thick with rage and the thirst for revenge.

"No." I stop him. "You put me in charge of her, Oz. You have to let me do this my way."

"This man is threatening *me*. And my *family*." Oz's anger brooks no argument. But fuck it. I know the way this has to go. And I'm not taking no for an answer.

"No," I repeat, louder this time. "Not your club. Mine."

"Yours?" His tone makes it clear he's about to refuse.

"It has to be the Lords for this to work, Oz." I'm not going to budge on this, and he needs to know it. "I've fought with them. Bled with them. I know my brothers, and they know me. If you throw men we haven't worked with into it, you put all of us in danger. Including Isabel."

Oz is silent, weighing my words. I'm almost sure he's going to continue arguing. But some star must be looking down on me for once in my life, because he ends up relenting.

"You'll get Isabel out of there before this happens. I don't want her put at risk," he warns. It's not a question.

"Of course. She'll be safe. I give you my word."

It's a small lie. But it doesn't matter. I *do* intend to keep Isabel safe, no matter what. Beyond that, Oz doesn't need to know anything else. All he needs to know is, I'm going to take care of Fowler, for good. Me and my club.

"All right," he finally growls. "But I do not think I have to tell you what the consequences will be if this goes bad."

It's a threat. More than that, it's a promise.

If this goes wrong, the alliance between our clubs will be broken.

I may pay for it with my life.

Most importantly, though: *Isabel* will be hurt. Raped, for sure. Probably killed.

But I *know* — I know it in my bones — that I'm the best shot of her staying alive.

And if Isabel is killed, I don't want to live, anyway.

"No," I say. "You don't."

I ring Rock from a clean burner. My prez hasn't heard from me in a while, so I spend some time filling him in on the details of what I know. I tell him our location, and what I want to put in place to catch Fowler and his men.

"You're expecting Fowler to show up himself?" Rock asks.

"Yeah. Hoping. And I'm guessing he'll have men with him, but if we're lucky he won't suspect anything. Still, we'll need as many Lords as you can spare. And they'll need to get up here without being followed. I'd bet money Fowler has people watching the club."

Rock grunts. "And when we get up there?"

"We kill them. Fowler first, and everyone else with him."

If I expect any pushback from Rock, I don't get it. Instead, I can practically hear his grin through the phone.

"Been a little quiet around here since you've been gone, Thorn," he chuckles. "Looks like that's about to end. I'll call church and tell the Lords what to get ready for. Phone me back tomorrow morning and we'll get everything in place."

27
ISABEL

Thorn is outside on the porch, talking to my father. The conversation's heated, and loud enough that I can hear a lot of what's being said on this end even though I'm in the kitchen trying to pretend I'm not trying to listen in.

They're talking about Fowler, which I know is the name of the man who's looking for me to get to Oz. It sounds like they're arguing about a strategy to lure him out in the open and take him out. I've never actually heard anyone talk back to my father before. But Thorn isn't backing down. Eventually, they seem to come to some sort of agreement, and Thorn hangs up.

He comes back inside, looking preoccupied. It's a look I've seen on his face a lot in recent days. I want to ask him about the conversation, but something stops me. I don't want to upset the fragile state of complicity we've been in since last night. I don't want to do anything to make him angry, or doubt me.

In the end, though, I don't have to ask him to tell me what's going on.

"Isabel," he murmurs, taking my hand and pulling me to him. His eyes bore into mine. "I need to talk to you about something. A way to end this."

I look up at him, meeting his gaze without flinching. "It sounds serious."

"It is. Probably dangerous, too." His brow furrows. "But it might be the only way to eliminate the threat from Fowler once and for all."

My eyes are still locked on his. I want him to tell me everything. But even more importantly, I want him to know that I'm with him, whatever he decides to do. "Okay," I nod.

"Okay?"

"Okay," I repeat. "I trust you. I know you'll do whatever is right. Whatever's best. So, okay. I'll do anything you say, Thorn. Whatever you need for me to do."

Thorn just stares down at me, saying nothing. His eyes grow dark, then soft, and then something else that makes a little shiver run down my spine.

"You're quite something, you know that, Isabel?" he murmurs. His mouth comes down on mine. He kisses me deeply, passionately, and I open to him, my arms going around his neck to pull him closer. The kiss makes me dizzy with want, and when he finally breaks away from me, I'm panting.

"I thought you said you needed to *talk* to me," I gasp.

"First things first," he growls, lifting me up into his arms. He tosses me over his shoulder. "Talk later."

"I can walk, you know," I complain. "Caveman."

"You might not be able to walk when I'm done with you," he tosses back. He reaches up and swats me on the ass, and I yelp and start giggling as he carries me through the threshold into the bedroom.

But my giggles turn to moans when he sets me on my feet and pushes me against the wall. He kisses me again, harder this time, our tongues dancing and searching as he pulls off first my clothing and then his.

"I need to fuck you," he groans. He pulls me to him, one hand cupping my ass and pressing it against his hardness, the other going to my breast, teasing my already hardening nipple. I suck in a breath and stifle a moan.

"So, fuck me," I pant. He chuckles low in his throat.

"I'm about to. You're a fucking drug, Isabel, you know that? You're all I can think about. Your pussy clenching around my cock." His words start a throbbing of anticipation between my legs. "I fucking need this. I need you."

"Oh, God, Thorn…" I moan as his hardness rubs against me in just the right place. "God, I can't wait to have you inside me." I reach down and wrap my fingers around his length, my heart leaping as I hear him hiss. I'm soaking wet with desire, but before he does anything, I need to taste him. Locking eyes with him, I drop to my knees, my hand still wrapped around him, and take his head in my mouth. I slowly start to pump his base with my fist as I lick him, coating his cock with my saliva and sucking it like a lollipop.

"Jesus," he whispers, fisting a hand in my hair. I take him deeper, until he starts to hit the back of my throat, and start pumping him a little harder, a little faster. "Touch yourself," he commands. With my other hand, I do as I'm told, sliding two fingers between my soaking folds. The sensation makes me shudder, and I moan against his cock. The vibrations make Thorn groan softly. "Fuck, that feels good," he tells me.

I think he's going to let me keep going, let me make him come like that, but he pulls away after a couple of minutes. At my whimper of disappointment, he chuckles low in his throat. "Sorry, darlin', but I seem to remember telling you I was gonna fuck you. A man's only as good as his word, after all." I start to take my hand away from my pussy, but he shakes his head sternly. "Ah, no. I didn't tell you to stop that, did I?"

"But…" I murmur uncertainly. I've never done… *that*… in front of anyone. But I know Thorn wants what he wants. He reaches down and pulls me up until I'm standing in front of him, then turns me so I'm facing the dresser. He bends me over so I'm bracing myself against it, and positions himself behind me. "Keep going, Isabel," he murmurs against my ear. One hand comes around my waist and places itself on top of mine. He uses two of my fingers and begins to stroke my clit in a circular motion, using my slick juices to tease me. With his other hand, he spreads my legs and then slides his head against my wet opening. He enters me from behind as he continues to use my fingers to stroke me. The angle of his cock presses against the front of my channel, and as he begins to thrust, he rolls his hips to hit the spot he found before that drives me wild.

My pleasure mounts quickly, and I whimper his name over and over as I hold on for dear life and lose myself in the bliss. His rhythm increases, his thrusts getting harder and more insistent, and I feel myself climbing higher and higher until finally I cry out, my climax bursting over me so powerfully it takes my breath away. Soon after, Thorn lets go of my hand and grips both of my hips hard. He pumps deeper and deeper, until with a shout he releases a hot stream of his seed deep inside me. As he shudders, he reaches up and turns my face to his, his tongue forcing its way into my mouth.

We breathe raggedly against each other, our bodies rising and falling in rhythm.

"You trust me," he murmurs against my throat.

"I trust you," I tell him, the words coming from deep inside me. "More than anyone, Thorn. More than anyone, ever."

Later, we lie in bed, with me pressed tight against him. Thorn tells me about his plan.

"We can take down Fowler," he says. "This needs to end. So you can be free. So it can all be over."

He explains what he wants to do, and what my role will be in all of it. Crazily, even though I should be scared, what I feel most is a strange, almost painful pang of regret. Because once this is all over, Thorn and I will leave this place. And once that happens, I'll probably never see him again.

A wave of sadness washes over me. But I try my best not to let him see it.

"You know I'll keep you safe, Isabel. Don't you?" he murmurs gently, raising my chin toward his with a finger. "You know I'll never let anything happen to you."

"Yes," I say without hesitation. Because I do know it, as surely as I know anything. Thorn will never let me get hurt. I don't question that for a second. So even though I am just a little afraid, and a lot sad, I'll do what I can to help him. I'll do whatever he says.

And most of all, I'll be brave. Because that's what he needs me to be.

28
THORN

Over the next several days, I coordinate with the Lords and Oz to set up the ambush. There's no way to predict exactly when Fowler will drive up here — or even if he will — but I'm banking that he's frustrated enough by now he'll take off as soon as his mole feeds him the intel on where Isabel is.

Isabel was the one who had the idea to try to work it for a Sunday. She remembered what the lady who checked us in said about the lodge office being closed. And we definitely want to keep this shit as on the down low as possible. The last fucking thing we need is any civilians getting caught in the crossfire.

We're in luck as far as that's concerned. I've done some recon around the area and there's still no other guests staying at any of the other cabins here as far as I can see. We're as alone as we can be.

The Lords come out in small groups over the course of a couple days, to avoid detection. They make their way here in roundabout fashion, and arrive in the dead of night, hiding their vehicles far from sight of the lodge. They bring food and supplies with them, and sleep rough on the floor of the cabin. Isabel meets them one by one, and if she's bothered by sharing her living quarters with so many men she takes it in stride.

When all of the brothers Rock sent me are assembled, we crowd into the main room of the cabin to hold an impromptu session of church. Rock's not here, having stayed behind to avoid suspicion. Isabel goes to the fridge and grabs bottles of beer for everyone, going around the room to pass them around. When she's finished, she slides down onto the floor next to the edge of the couch where I'm sitting.

Angel calls the meeting to order. As he does, a couple of the men glance over at Isabel and frown.

"She gonna stay here for this?" Sarge asks, a look of disapproval on his face.

Ghost, our Sergeant at Arms, cuts his eyes at him sharply. "She's involved in this. Her life's on the line, too. Of course she should be here."

"Isabel is agreeing to play decoy to lure that fucker here, Sarge," I half-snarl. "You think she doesn't have a right to know what the goddamn plan is?"

"Jesus, okay! Okay!" Sarge raises his hands. "It's just a little weird to have snatch sitting in on church."

At the mention of the word *snatch*, it's like a bomb explodes inside me. I'm up off the couch and across the room in seconds, my hand around his throat.

"Apologize," I hiss. Sarge's face turns confused, then angry. I tighten my grip on his throat. "*Now*."

Sarge makes a choking sound in his throat, but his eyes turn defiant. "Looks like living with pussy's turned you soft, Thorn," he rasps.

The crack of my fist hitting his face resounds through the room.

In an instant, all hell breaks loose.

Men are up out of their seats. Bottles fall to the floor. I've got Sarge down on the ground. He's strong, and probably has a few pounds on me, but I've got the element of surprise and I'm also fucking mad as hell. He's no match for me as he simultaneously tries to land a punch and throw me off him. I block his hand with my left arm and, tucking my chin, head butt him in the face as he tries to rise.

"Fuck!" he yells. Blood spatters from his mouth. I raise my fist to hammer him again, but then I'm being pulled off him by a couple of the brothers.

"Thorn, Thorn!" Angel shouts. "Let it go! We've got shit to do here. This ain't the time, or the place."

I look around wildly to see who's got hold of me. To my left, Gunner's yanking back on my arm. To my right, Beast is staring me down.

"Leave it, brother," he says simply.

I shake them off and take a step back. Sarge is sitting in a wooden straight-back chair, bleeding profusely from his face. He gives me a bloody sneer but says nothing.

Beast leans in toward me. "What the fuck, Thorn?" he asks quietly. "You claimin' her?"

I dodge the question. I'm breathing heavily, less from exertion than from seething anger that's still boiling just below the surface. "Isabel is off limits," I announce. "To *everyone*." I look around the room, meeting every man's eyes in turn. "And you'll fucking treat her with respect."

Angel cuts in. "All right. Let's move on. We've got business to attend to. I'm in charge here, and Isabel stays."

That seems to cut through the bullshit. One by one, the men sit back down. Isabel goes to the kitchen and comes back with a roll of paper towels, which she wordlessly hands to Sarge. I try not to smirk as he takes them from her and pulls off a few to hold to his bleeding face. She comes back toward me and sits down on the floor again next to me. I look down at her. Her eyes are glistening. She gives me the tiniest of smiles.

"The idea is that Isabel will be alone in the house," I'm saying as I look around the room. "By herself. She'll have a burner phone with my number in case she needs it. And pepper spray, in case she needs to incapacitate him before we can get to her."

Isabel makes a tiny noise in her throat. Looking down, I'm struck by how pale she is. But then she turns her face up to meet my gaze, and nods bravely. I reach down and give her shoulder a reassuring squeeze.

"We'll be out of sight, in the woods, planted strategically all around the cabin. We'll need to leave plenty of time so there's no chance of any of us still being close to the house when Fowler arrives. So we're looking at a few hours out in the cold."

Gunner grins. "No worries. We've all been through worse than that."

"How many men you think Fowler will have with him, Thorn?" Angel asks me.

"Hard to say. But the story Oz is feeding his mole is that Isabel's bodyguard abandoned her, and that she's been out here alone for a couple of days. She's scared, and alone, and called Daddy to send one of his men to come pick her up." I frown. "So, I don't expect him to come alone, but we're hoping he's not bringing more than a few men for protection."

"You think she ought to have a gun on her?" Hawk asks, nodding toward Isabel.

"We've talked about it," I reply. "But Isabel says she's not comfortable with that. And in any case, I think Fowler's gonna be more concerned with, uh, *toying* with her a little bit before he would want to kill her." Beside me, Isabel flinches, but says nothing. "This is what I've understood from Oz, anyway. It's his M.O."

"That sick fuck," Brick, our Enforcer, seethes.

"If Isabel plays her role right, he won't be expecting her to defend herself. The pepper spray should be all she needs to immobilize him until we can get to him." I nod toward the woods outside. "To be fully out of sight, we'll need to be at least a quarter-mile away. When I get the call from Isabel, that means she'll have about ninety seconds alone with him until we get here."

"You sure you don't want to have someone in the house with her?" Angel asks.

"No." Isabel speaks up, her voice loud and clear. "If what my father tells Thorn is correct, Fowler's an intelligent man. If he senses anything at all is up, he's likely to act unpredictably. We don't want him to suspect a thing. And for that to work, there has to be nothing for him to suspect."

"I don't like this," Beast mutters.

"It's what she wants, brother. And for the record, I think she's right."

And I do. It's the smartest way to go. The best shot we have at trapping Fowler and giving him every second of the long, drawn out and painful death he deserves. But fuck, I don't like it, either. Every cell in my body is screaming at me not to leave Isabel alone for one fucking second. There's a voice yelling in my head, telling me I'm insane, telling me to stop this nonsense and take her far away from here, far away from everything.

But the rational part of me — the part I'm trying hard to listen to — tells me that if I do that, Isabel will never be safe again. Not as long as Fowler is alive. Men like him don't let jobs go unfinished. They don't abandon plans to fuck with someone once they've decided someone needs to be fucked with.

I might be making the biggest mistake of my fucking life, doing this.

But I won't let that mistake be because I hesitated to do what needed to be done. I can't let my emotions stop me. Fowler must be killed. All decisions need to point to the surest way toward that result.

But if this is a mistake — if anything happens to Isabel because of this decision — it'll be the last mistake I ever make. I'll make sure of that myself.

In the end, Beast manages to convince Isabel to let him leave a small, light pistol in a small drawer of the bathroom vanity. "Just in case, darlin'," he drawls. "You never know."

I suspect she agrees to it just so he'll let it go. But I have to admit, it makes me feel a little easier knowing it's there. Isabel assures me she knows how to use it, and promises me she will if she has to.

That night, the men seek out corners and bits of floor to lie down and catch some rest. A few of them go into the second bedroom and fight it out for one of the bunk beds. Isabel and I go to the main bedroom and close the door behind us. I savor the moment of aloneness with her. It's one of the last moments we'll have before this all goes down. The calm before the storm.

"Are you sure you're ready for this?" I ask her, as we lie together in the dark. I feel her nod and snuggle deeper against me. My chest constricts as I think about leaving her in just a few short hours. It's possible — though I tell myself it's not likely — that one of us might not make it out of this alive.

I pray to God it's not Isabel.

"Thorn?" her voice is small.

"Yes, darlin'," I answer.

"I'm a little bit scared."

"I know you are." I pull her closer. "That's good. Fear is important. It sharpens your senses."

"You're just saying that," she murmurs.

"No. I'm not." I kiss the top of her head. "If you don't let it get the best of you, fear is what keeps you alert. It's what keeps you focused. You know what to do, Isabel. You just have to stay focused, and do it. I'll be there to save you. You know that, right?"

"Yes." She's emphatic.

"Well, then. We just have to get through the next few hours, don't we? After that, it'll all be over."

Isabel is silent for a second. "What then?" she whispers.

Then, I'll take you back to Tanner Springs and make you mine.

Then, I'll tell Oz he can go fuck himself if he thinks I'm ever letting you go.

Then, I'll lock you up in my own house, and keep you with me and out of danger for the rest of your days.

I clear my throat.

"Then," I say hoarsely, "I take you far away from this place, and fuck you until neither of us can walk."

About three in the morning, my burner phone buzzes on the nightstand next to me.

It's Oz. When I pick up, he tells me the one thing I've been waiting to hear. And the one thing I've been dreading.

"Playboy has left the area," he says. "He left town an hour ago."

I end the call and slide silently out of bed. Pulling on my jeans, I go out into the main room and rouse Angel.

"It's time," I say.

29
THORN

An hour or so after I get the call from Oz, we run into an unexpected complication.

It starts to snow.

"We need to move," I murmur to Angel as the men ready themselves. "We need to leave time to be sure our tracks are completely covered before anyone shows up."

"True," he nods. "This could actually end up working to our advantage. It will be more convincing that Isabel's truly alone out here if the snow around the cabin is obviously undisturbed."

We may have a long wait out in the woods ahead of us. Thankfully, the temps are only in the low thirties. Assuming Fowler shows up sometime today, we'll be fine. Angel tells everyone we're heading out, and ten minutes later, the Lords slip outside into the early morning half-light.

Isabel's up with us, of course. I stand with her as we watch my brothers file out the door in pairs. I know within minutes, they'll all be in place, in the formation we discussed last night.

"This is it," I murmur to her as Angel and Brick, the last two, file out the door. "I'd better get out there."

"I know." She looks up at me. Her face is still pale, but her jaw is set. Determined.

"You gonna be all right?"

She nods, a little too quickly. "I'll be okay." She inhales a shaky breath, then lets it out noisily. "I have everything I need." She pats the back pockets of her jeans. "I'll have the phone ready to call you at the first sign."

"We'll probably see them before you do," I promise. "But this way, I'll know you're in place and ready to go."

Isabel nods. She takes another deep breath, shivering a little. "Good luck, Thorn."

I start to reply, but the words catch in my throat. Instead, I pull her to me. My lips find hers. I kiss her long, and hard, hard enough that we'll both carry the memory of it with us. When I pull away, her eyes are shining.

"I'll see you on the other side," I say, my voice hoarse.

"Okay," she whispers with a tremulous smile.

Ten minutes later, we're all in position. It's snowing harder now, which means our tracks will be gone within the hour. From my spot behind a downed tree deep in the woods, I stare at the little house, with its single warm light coming from the living room. I think about Isabel in there, all alone, and ache to be with her.

I know she's as safe as she possibly can be right now, given the circumstances. The house is surrounded on all sides by Lords. In my gut, I know it will be okay. But if I'm wrong — if anything happens to her, anything at all — I'll never forgive myself for it. Because after all, I'm the one that set this up. I'm the one who put her in there, all by herself, as bait for the man we're after.

We wait, and then we wait some more. The cold isn't too bad, but it's tough not to be able to move around much. We could be here for hours, maybe all day. Shit, maybe longer than that. Now that we're committed to this course of action, our only choice is to wait. I can't even smoke, because the smell might alert Fowler's men that there's someone here. My mind travels back to the first day at Connegut with Isabel. I remember how she wrinkled her nose and asked if I had to smoke inside.

Maybe it's time to cut down.

The thought takes me by surprise. I know smoking's bad for you, but I've never much cared. If today goes as planned though, maybe it's time to start thinking more long-term. After all, I can't protect Isabel if I'm not around.

The Lords keep communication to a minimum except when necessary. I hear the occasional rustle in the trees that tells me when one of them is changing position, or going out for a piss. About eleven o'clock in the morning, the snow finally starts to abate. I look down at the footprints I made when I trudged into the trees to get into place: there's no sign of them at all.

Suddenly, there's a buzz in my back pocket. I've been sitting here so long that it startles the shit out of me. Suppressing a curse, I grab the mobile and look at the screen. It's a text from Ghost, who's stationed further up the road with Hawk and Sarge. *There's a car coming.*

Half a minute later, a slow-moving SUV with darkened windows comes rolling into view. I'm too far away and too well covered to be seen, but just the same I crouch down behind the fallen tree, lifting my head up just far enough to see the progress of the vehicle. Its tires crunch in the new fallen snow, the sound deepening as the car slows and then turns into the drive toward the cabin.

My chilled fingers work awkwardly as I tap out a message to Isabel: *They're here.*

A second later comes her response: *K.*

Slowly and silently, I move myself into a crouching position and glance over to my left, where Beast is stationed about fifty feet away from me. I wait until he turns toward me and nod once, lifting my hand: *Wait.* He nods back. Then I see him turn in the other direction and do the same to his left, where Angel should be.

I watch as the SUV stops, the door opens, and four men get out. One of them, in the passenger side, is older and slightly smaller than the rest. He hangs back, waiting for the others to surround him before they go further.

Fowler.

What happens next is the hardest thing I've ever done in my life.

I watch, not moving, as they draw their guns for cover and push inside the front door.

My heart is fucking pounding in my chest as I force myself not to act until the door closes behind them.

I make myself count. *One. Two. Three.*

Then, turning to Beast, I raise my hand and chop toward the cabin. *Move.*

Beast, Angel and I move silently toward the house. Gunner and Brick stay behind in the trees, each armed with an AR-15 just in case we get more company.

When we're positioned around the house, I slide under the window that we've left cracked open off the front room. A deep male voice is speaking, followed by Isabel's, high-pitched and tense. God damn it, I want to go in there right now and shoot that son of a bitch in the head. It takes everything in me to wait, to make sure the moment's right.

"Are you my dad's men?" she's asking tremulously. "He said he'd come and get me and bring me home!"

Fowler fucking *laughs*, and the perverse sound twists in my gut. "Your father can't help you. He thinks he's a goddamn genius. Untouchable. But the man's a fool."

"Who are you then?" I can hear the rising fear in her voice even from here. God, Isabel deserves a freaking award for this acting. Fowler's buying it hook, line, and sinker.

I risk a quick glance through the window. Isabel's standing right at the entrance to the hallway, between the kitchen and the living room. She's positioned herself perfectly. The men with Fowler have lowered their guns, apparently convinced she's alone and vulnerable.

"I'm someone your father wronged. Very badly," Fowler says, his tone ice-cold. "And you… are about to pay for his sins."

I take out my phone and type a single word. One she won't see until later. But the word doesn't matter. What matters is the silent vibration of the phone in her back pocket. The one that will tell her it's time to act.

Now.

Right on cue, Isabel takes a step backward, reaching back as though she's feeling faint and about to grab the wall behind her for support. The eyes of Fowler and his two men are focused on her, and more importantly, away from the door. But instead of bracing herself against the wall, she brings one hand forward with the pepper spray and shoots a stream of it right at Fowler's face before he can react.

Quick as a flash, Isabel turns and bolts down the hallway. Fowler starts to scream, but he's choked off by a fit of violent coughing. He doubles over in pain, and starts to claw frantically at his face. A couple of his men begin coughing, too, less violently. The one who's least affected draws his gun and runs after Isabel. Fowler shouts after him.

"Don't harm her!" he rages. "She's *mine*!"

I hear a muffled slam, and know Isabel's reached the bathroom and locked herself in.

I look over at my brothers and nod. As one, we storm the front door and into the house, weapons drawn.

"Drop your guns!" I shout. "Now! *Now!*"

We have the element of surprise, but Fowler's men are well trained. Fowler himself stumbles toward the bedroom, out of the line of fire. Two of his men turn and take aim, one of them at me. The third runs down the hall and cuts into the second bedroom — the one closest to the bathroom where Isabel's locked herself in. I dodge behind the couch, but one of them manages to clip me in the left shoulder, making me drop the gun in my left hand. More gunshots ring out. I flatten myself on the ground behind the couch and strain my hand toward my Sig, barely managing to reach it and still stay out of sight.

Pain flashes in my shoulder, but I don't think the wound is that bad, so I ignore it. I pull myself to the other side and peer around the couch. The fucker who shot me is on the ground, bleeding from a wound to the chest. Everything else is fucking chaos. Beast is nowhere in sight so I think he's followed either Fowler or the third guy. Angel's got his guy against the counter in the kitchen, working on wrestling the gun from his hand. The fucker fires wildly, hitting the ceiling, and then with a yell manages to shove Angel just enough to catch him off balance. But Angel grabs hold and takes the piece of shit down with him.

I hear sounds of a fight in the second bedroom. I stagger up and into the hallway. The main bedroom door is closed, and I take aim and fire at the lock. The flimsy door splinters on the bullet's impact. When I kick in what's left of it the room's empty, the window open.

I run across the room and look out. The snow on the ground is disturbed, and Fowler's nowhere in sight. "Fuck!" I shout, stuffing my piece into my waistband. I grip the sill, hoisting myself through the opening and dropping down into the snow below. I can't take the chance that Gunner and Brick will miss their shots at him. Fowler cannot escape.

The tracks lead toward the front side of the house. I pull my gun and run in that direction, and round the corner just in time to hear Fowler start the engine of the SUV. I take aim and fire at the front tire. It just misses the rubber. Fowler throws the SUV into reverse, flooring it. I change angles and fire again. The bullet shatters the front windshield. From the corner of my eye, I see Gunner and Brick coming through the trees. Brick drops to his knees and takes aim, then fires off ten rounds, riddling the side panel with bullets. One of them hits the gas tank. The car swerves, but keeps going. It's almost too far away from me now, but as a last attempt, I raise my Sig and fire into the cab.

I only know I've hit him when the SUV lurches wildly, careening off the gravel driveway and smashing its back end into a tree. "Grab him!" I yell to Gunner and Brick, and turn back toward the house. Just as I do, a single shot rings out from inside.

I bolt for the door. Inside, Beast and Angel are standing in the living room, two bodies in a pile between them. A third one is crumpled in the hallway.

But what makes my blood run to ice is what I see next.

The bathroom door.

With a bullet hole through it.

"Isabel!" I shout, bolting past the men down the hall. "Jesus, Isabel, are you hurt? Answer me, baby!"

"Thorn!" comes the muffled cry from the other side.

I jump over the body lying in my way and shout at her to open the door. But just the knob begins to turn, I see something that stops me in my tracks.

The wood shrapnel is on *this* side.

The door opens. Isabel is staring at me, wide-eyed.

On the sink next to her is Beast's .9mm.

"Holy shit, babe," I breathe, turning toward the hallway. "Did you shoot that guy?"

"She sure as hell did."

I look over and Angel is grinning at the two of us.

"Fuckin' badass," he smirks nodding toward her.

I turn back to Isabel. She bites her lip and risks a small smile.

"Jesus, woman!" I start laughing crazily. "Remind me never to make you mad again!"

Just then, the cunt Isabel shot groans softly. He's not dead, yet. I bend down to take a look at his wound. Isabel got him in the gut, and he's bleeding pretty bad. He's the scrawniest one of the bunch, with a hawk nose and a greasy ponytail. He's not wearing any colors, but I catch a glimpse of a familiar tattoo through a rip in his T-shirt.

Death Devils.

This must be Playboy.

"You better hope you don't survive this, motherfucker," I hiss down at him. "If Oz gets his hands on you, you'll be begging for a swift death."

Just then Gunner comes jogging through the front door. "We got Fowler," he announces. "He's not gonna make it, but he's still breathing, for now."

I stand up and reach out my hand to Isabel. She takes it, and together, we follow Gunner back outside toward the crashed SUV.

Brick is standing beside it, his AR in his hand. A figure is slumped over the steering wheel, blood soaking his chest. His breathing is labored, as though he's barely able to suck in the little air he can get.

"So you're the infamous Fowler," I snarl. "Lot of trouble we went through, for such a goddamn pussy."

He wheezes, in… out… in. "Fuck… you," he finally manages.

"That's all you've got?" I throw back my head and laugh. "You stupid motherfucker." I pull out my gun and aim it straight at his head. Behind me, Isabel gasps. "I should end you right now, you waste of air," I continue. "But the lady has been through enough today, without adding seeing pieces of your skull spattered through this cab. Besides, I'm going to enjoy knowing you spent your final moments gasping for breath and knowing you fucking failed."

Fowler's eyes are full of hate.

It makes me happy.

"Goodbye, you piece of shit," I tell him. "Enjoy your eternity in an unmarked grave."

Turning away from the SUV, I look at Gunner and Brick. "Looks like we've got some cleanup to do."

"We'll take care of it," Brick says. Gunner nods. "Why don't you get Isabel back home. Like you said, she's been through enough for today."

"Thanks, brothers," I say sincerely. Gunner claps me on the back. Brick shakes my hand.

"Congratulations, little lady," Gunner says with a wink at Isabel. "You're safe."

"Thank you so much," she breathes. Her voice is still a little shaky. "Thank all of you."

"Don't mention it." Brick rumbles.

"You goin' back to Tanner Springs?" Gunner asks me then. "I think Alix would like to meet the girl she sent those clothes to. She's been askin' me about her, wanting to know how she is and if she's okay."

I glance over at Isabel. She's looking at me, waiting for my answer.

"Yeah," I nod. "We're going back to the clubhouse. I think it's time she meets everyone else."

THORN

* * *

In the end, Playboy didn't make it long enough for us to bring him back to Oz. When he goes to meet his maker, he should thank Him for that kindness.

I rang Oz from the road, when we were stopped at a gas station so Isabel could go to the bathroom. I told him Isabel was safe, and that Fowler, Playboy and the others were dead.

I also told him Isabel was my old lady now, and that if he needed to have words with me about it, that was fine.

Oz didn't say anything for a couple of seconds. In the end, he told me we'd talk later. I took that as a good sign.

When Isabel comes back from the gas station bathroom, she's looking a little less shell-shocked. If you didn't know her, or everything that had just happened to her, you'd assume she was just a girl on a road trip with her man.

Her man, who is absolutely off his head crazy about her.

"I spoke to Oz," I tell her when she's back in the car.

"Let me guess. The first thing he asked about was whether you had Fowler and Playboy for him."

"No, actually. He asked about you straightaway. He was relieved as shit you're okay. 'Course, I neglected to tell him you were a little closer to the action than I had originally let on."

"So, I'm never going to get to tell Dad that I'm — what did Gunner call me? A badass?"

"A *fuckin'* badass," I correct her. "And no, not unless you want him to murder me."

Isabel flashes me a grin that's so normal — so fucking *normal* — that it just about breaks my heart.

"I guess I wouldn't want to risk that," she teases. "I've gotten kind of used to you."

"That right?" I grin back.

"Yeah. But don't press your luck." She gives me a sly wink.

I can't help but laugh. "Noted."

"Anyways," Isabel says, leaning back in her seat with a sigh, "my father would never believe it if we told him. Oz thinks I'm nothing but a helpless little flower. Always has."

"He doesn't know you very well, then." I reach over and take her hand, looking her in the eye. "After today, I'm not sure you ever needed my protection in the first place. You're the bravest person I know, Isabel Mandias."

And the funny thing is…

It's true.

30
ISABEL

By the time we get back to Tanner Springs, it's already late. Predictably, Thorn drives the whole way and doesn't let me get behind the wheel. I give him shit about it, but truthfully I'm exhausted, and more than ready to let him take control.

Instead of driving to the clubhouse, he takes me straight to his house. "We'll go to the clubhouse tomorrow, after we've both had some rest," he says as he leads me up the driveway.

It's dark, and the street he lives on is mostly deserted, though there are cars in the driveways and lights on in most of the houses. It's funny, we've been more or less alone for so long that it's sort of strange to be back in civilization again. I'm actually relieved that we're not going into a rowdy clubhouse full of drinking, shouting, and screwing. I know from experience with my dad's club what men like the Lords are like when they're all together. I think I need a little more time to get ready for that.

This is the fourth place I've been holed up with Thorn since the night Oz's men kidnapped me at the roadhouse. But it's the first time I've ever been in a space that belongs to him. Sleepy as I am, I can't help but look around for clues about the man I've just spent the last month with. The walls of his entry way and living room are painted a deep burgundy, with a large, overstuffed leather sofa to match in one corner. The furniture is all low to the ground and comfortable-looking. There are very few knickknacks, save for a few pictures on a credenza by the window. I resist the urge to go look at them; I hope I'll have a chance later, when Thorn's eyes aren't on me.

"How are you doing?" Thorn asks, coming up from behind to wrap his arms around me. "Tired?"

"Yeah," I admit, stifling a yawn.

"*Too* tired?"

I crane my neck to look back at him. One side of his mouth is curved into a devilish grin.

"Why, Thorn, I'm sure I don't know what you mean!" I tease him, as heat begins to pool in my belly. "Are you suggesting perhaps doing a load of laundry? I sure could use some clean clothes…"

I never get a chance to finish the sentence as Thorn picks me up unceremoniously and tosses me over his shoulder.

With a yelp, I pretend to beat on his back, kicking my legs as he carries me down his hallway.

"You have got to stop with this caveman thing!" I protest. Even though I don't mean it. Not even a little bit.

Thorn makes love to me that night. It's different from how it's been every other time with him. Not less passionate. Not less raw. Maybe even more raw. But under the rawness, there's a tenderness. A fullness, an intensity that comes from the fact that both of us could have died today, but we didn't. And now we're here, having been through that crucible together.

Together.

"I couldn't have stood losing you back there, Sibéal," he whispers against my ear when we're lying back against the sheets, after an orgasm that shook both of us to the core at the same time. "You were a fucking marvel, you know that?"

"It was because of you, Thorn." I shiver a little as his breath teases my skin. "I knew you'd never let anything happen to me. I knew you'd keep me safe. I knew we would get through it."

He holds me against him so tightly I have a little trouble breathing, but it feels so good, so *solid*. I've never felt so whole and real before. I don't know how he does that. For maybe the first time in my life, I feel anchored to something. I reach up and finger the little starfish necklace, and think of my mom. I wonder if she'd like Thorn.

I wonder if she'll ever get a chance to meet him.

A lump forms in my throat, but I force it down, force myself to ignore it. Right now, all I want is to be here with him. I don't want the past, or the future, to intrude. All I want is the present.

Because right now, the present is more wonderful than anything I ever could have imagined.

* * *

The next day dawns bright and sunny. The sky is that clear, crystalline blue that it sometimes gets in the winter, but amazingly the temperature is unseasonably warm.

When I open my eyes, Thorn's already up and out of bed. Like the first morning at the safe house, I can smell bacon and coffee wafting toward me. A grin spreads across my face as I remember that day, and think about how much has changed since then.

I look around Thorn's bedroom for the first time in the light. The walls are a slate gray, but the bed comforter and all the bedding is a stark, fluffy white. His cut is lying on a chair next to the dresser. My clothing is pooled on the floor.

I pull on my jeans and T-shirt and pad out into the kitchen. Thorn's pouring a cup of coffee, whistling to himself.

"Weatherman says we're in for a warm snap, next few days," he rumbles. He hands me the cup, which I take gratefully. "I thought we could take the bike to the clubhouse."

"Sounds good to me," I nod. I take a sip of the coffee. It's strong, but good.

"Gunner called a bit ago," he continues. "Sounds like some of the old ladies got it into their heads to do a barbecue today, since it'll be nice out." He glances over at me with a sexy grin. "You up for that?"

I smile back at him. "You give me some of that bacon, I'll do anything you say."

"Anything, eh?" He wiggles his brows at me.

I snort. "Mr. O'Malley, you do not need to bribe me with bacon for *that*."

After a late breakfast — and a rather *long* shower — we get dressed and ready to go to the clubhouse. I'm nervous, not because I'm afraid of the MC — after all, I've been around motorcycle clubs my whole life — but because for some reason, I feel like making a good impression on these men is almost a test. At least I've met a few of them by now, and I think Beast and Gunner, at least, don't hate me. But I'm going to their territory now. Their turf. And if I know anything about MCs, it's that each one has its own culture. And it's up to me to adapt, not the other way around.

Thorn fires up his Harley and wheels it out of his garage, motioning for me to get on the back. I do so, and wrap my arms around his waist as I put my feet on the pegs. We take off, and I shiver a little at the cold air and press myself into his back. This is my first time in Tanner Springs, so I have plenty to look at as we ride through town. *This is where Thorn lives.* This is where his life is. It's strange, imagining him here all these years. I was not even two hours away, living my own life. Telling myself the one thing I wanted was to get as far away from the Death Devils and my father as possible.

Yet here I am. In love with a member of a rival MC. Hoping against hope that today doesn't mark the end of my time with Thorn.

I squeeze my eyes shut tight against the thought. For the dozenth time since we arrived here, I will myself to not have any expectations. To try as hard as I can to enjoy every minute with Thorn, for whatever it's worth. With my eyes closed, it's easier to feel the vibrations and motions of the bike. It's funny: as a little girl, I was fascinated by motorcycles because of my father. Then as I got older, I hated them because of him. They've always been a symbol of raw, masculine power to me. But also of a world where I was practically invisible, excluded, and meant next to nothing. But here, on the bike with Thorn, I love the ride. The thrill of it. The exhilaration and feeling of freedom that you could never get by riding in a cage.

All too soon, Thorn pulls up at a large, flat-roofed warehouse-type structure. He pulls into the lot and parks his bike at the end of a long row of Harleys. Off to the side, there's an area with picnic tables, a large grill, and some kids' bikes strewn around. I hop off and wait for him to set it down on the kickstand.

"Ready?" he asks me as he stands.

As ready as I'll ever be. "Yep." I nod.

Thorn reaches out his hand, and I take it. My heart jumps practically into my throat, and I try not to jump to conclusions about what it means. We enter the clubhouse together. I have to remember to keep breathing in and out instead of holding my breath.

We're barely inside the door when a loud chorus of shouts greets us. Within seconds, we're surrounded by hard, tattooed men, all of them wearing the Lords of Carnage colors on their cuts. They take turns clapping Thorn on the back and giving him bear hugs. A few of them, the ones I recognize from yesterday, hang back and grin, nodding a silent hello at me. I wave back shyly and smile as I remember their names one by one: Angel, the club's vice-president. Gunner, with his dark hair and flashing blue eyes. Beast, the giant of the group. Ghost, Hawk, Sarge.

Once my eyes adjust more to the light, I realize there aren't only men here. A half-dozen women come up to us, turning to me with a smile. "Isabel!" one of them says. She has light brown eyes and beautiful, shoulder-length blond hair. "I'm Alix, Gunner's old lady!"

"Alix! Oh my gosh, you're the one who sent me up all the clothes and the Kindle!" I grab her hand and squeeze it impulsively.

"The very one!" she beams, and looks down at the shirt I'm wearing. I giggle, realizing it's actually hers. "Looks like I did okay on sizes," she winks, "Except you fill that shirt out a little better than I do!"

I laugh, and shake my head. "You have no idea how much I appreciated everything you sent me," I gush. "Especially the Kindle. I think you might have saved my sanity."

"I'm so glad!" she grins. "All I knew was, when Gunner told me Thorn was guarding someone at the safe house, I tried to imagine what the hell you were going to do all alone up there for days on end."

"Looks like she found *something* to do," the woman beside her smirks, nodding toward Thorn. She's got gorgeous deep red hair and hazel eyes. "Or some*one* to do, that is."

Before I can try to answer, Alix rolls her eyes. "This nosey one is Sydney," she says, nodding toward the redhead. "She's with Brick, the one over there." I look in the direction she's pointing, and recognize the large, heavily-tattooed man with black hair cut in a military style who was with us at the cabin at the end.

"Damn…" I murmur. The women all start laughing.

"Damn is right," Sydney winks. "I'd be telling you to back off right now, but given the way you and Thorn came in together, I don't think I need to worry."

"No kidding," agrees a third woman with long, dark brown hair. "I'm Samantha," she smiles. "I'm with Hawk."

"I'm Jenna, Ghost's wife," says a petite blonde. "And this is Jewel. She's the bartender here."

"Hi!" A tall, statuesque beauty with dark blond hair gives me a little wave.

"Hi," I say. I'm starting to get a little overwhelmed with names.

"So," the woman named Sydney says. "About Thorn!"

"Um…" I say, blushing. "I, uh…"

"Nope," Jenna shakes her head wryly. "*Um, uh* is not gonna be good enough. We're gonna need details. You just spent the better part of the month alone with that man. And it doesn't take a psychic to see that you spent your time doing more than playing checkers."

"I…" I stammer. "I mean…"

"Oh, boy. Jewel, this girl's gonna need some liquid courage," Jenna laughs, reaching over to loop her arm through mine. "Come on, Isabel. That big round table over there's where us old ladies do our talking. We'll get you loosened up. But I'll warn you right now, you won't be leaving your chair until we get you to spill. Even if we have to tie you up to do it."

Her words are so unintentionally perfect that I start laughing. "Ladies," I snort, "challenge accepted."

31
ISABEL

Hours later, I'm out in the back with the Lords, their old ladies, and a handful of kids who are running around like hellions. Somehow it feels like I've known these people practically my whole life. It might be due to the benefit of a couple of shots and a beer, but I can't remember the last time I felt so comfortable in a group of people.

The warm fuzzy sensation that I'm finally safe and among friends reminds me of something I've neglected to do for far too long. Stepping away from the group, I fish my half-broken phone out of my pocket and turn it on. Amazingly, it somehow still works after Thorn threw it against the wall. Smiling in relief, I peer through the broken glass of the screen and hit a number.

"Isabel?" Deb's voice is high-pitched and tearful when she answers. "Are you there?"

"Deb! Yes, it's me! I'm so sorry! I'm completely fine! I promise! I'm safe!"

"Oh, my God!" Deb instantly starts full-on crying. "Oh my God, Izzy, I was so worried! Where *are* you? I tried calling you so many times!"

"I'm in Tanner Springs," I tell her, choking up a little with love for my friend. "I'm totally okay. I just wanted to let you know. I promise I would have called you if I could have. I feel terrible — I know you were probably worried sick!"

"What *happened*?" she wails. "Where *were* you? When I came back to the bar with Ralph, you were just… gone!"

"It's a long story. But I promise to tell you about it just as soon as I get back to town." Then I remember something. "Oh, and I'm sorry about this, but I broke your heels."

Deb starts to laugh, half-hysterically. "Isabel, those were genuine Manolo knockoffs!"

I snort, filled with sudden warmth and relief that things are back to normal between us. "I promise to replace them with another pair next time we go shopping."

"When are you coming back?" she asks, sniffling a little.

I glance over at the group, my eyes sliding over people one by one until I spot Thorn.

"I'm not exactly sure," I admit. "I sort of… met someone. But it's a long story."

After I hang up with Deb, I go back to hang out with the old ladies. Thorn spends most of the afternoon catching up with the men, but from time to time our eyes meet. Each time, the look he gives me sends a jolt of heat straight through to my core. More than once, one of the women notices, and yet another round of good-natured teasing begins.

"I don't know what you did to Thorn, girl," Alix says, coming up next to me. "But it looks like you're gonna be a permanent fixture around here."

In spite of myself, a sudden rush of doubt hits me. "Do you really think so, Alix?" I ask her. I turn to her and decide to lay my cards on the table. "Because I'm pretty sure I'm in love with him."

She smiles at me kindly and shakes her head. "I would bet a mortgage payment on it," she grins. "He is *gone* on you. Are you seriously telling me you guys haven't even talked about this yet?"

"Not really," I murmur. "I mean, the last few days, there wasn't really time. And then after that…" I shrug. "I mean, I guess I was sort of afraid to bring anything up. I just…" I swallow painfully. "I just don't want this to end, you know?"

"Oh, girl, trust me." Alix laughs and puts an arm around me. "When a man like Thorn gets a look like *that* in his eye?

He's made up his mind. He just hasn't gotten around to telling you about it. But he will."

"I hope you're right," I say ruefully.

"I am." She nods. "And I'm glad. Thorn's a good man. He deserves someone like you. And it'll be good to have another old lady around here. These men can be a handful. We need each other to lean on."

I look over at Thorn, who's talking to Gunner, Beast, and Angel. "You've got that right," I grin.

A little later, Thorn disappears inside for a while. When he comes back, his eyes lock on mine and he heads straight for me.

"Well, it looks like Isabel's about to leave us for a little while, girls," Sydney announces, raising her beer.

"Sorry, ladies, I need to steal her from you for a bit," Thorn grins, and catches me around the waist.

"Bye, Isabel!" a couple of them hoot and call after me. "Enjoy the *ride*!"

"Oh, my gosh," I snort as Thorn leads me away. "Those ladies are not shy, are they?"

"They have strong personalities, that's for certain," he agrees, amused. "'Course, they'd have to have, to put up with this lot."

Thorn brings me inside the clubhouse, and takes me up some stairs to the second floor. I glance up at him, and notice his face is more relaxed than I've ever seen it. "You're glad to be back, aren't you?"

"Yeah." He nods once, chuckling. "Glad it's all over. And you're safe."

"It's nice to not have all that danger hanging over us, that's for sure."

We stop in front of a closed door. Thorn turns to me, hesitating. "I talked to Angel about the cleanup. After we left."

I haven't let myself think about that, but now that Thorn brings it up I can't help but ask.

"What about the bodies?" I say, shivering a little.

"Sorted," he nods. "And I thought you'd be happy to know, the brothers put some cash in an envelope and slipped it inside the mail slot in the door of the office." He gives me a grim smile. "As an incentive for the owners not to look much further into the damage."

I let out a breath. "That's good. I felt bad, leaving the cabin like that."

"The damage was pretty minimal. Apart from a few bullet holes, that is."

"I bet that's more excitement than the owners have ever had." I laugh ruefully, shaking my head.

"Likely," Thorn agrees. "Also, I went to talk to Rock, our prez, just now. He's the big, stocky, gruff-looking one. I wanted to let him know how everything ended up. And where we stand with the Death Devils."

"Oh?"

"Yeah. This bodyguard gig for Oz was a favor our club was doin' for him. A way to solidify the friendship between the two clubs."

"I see," I murmur, my heart sinking a little. "That's why you were doing it."

"Yeah. There was quite a bit riding on it." Thorn opens the door and nods for me to go in. It's a small apartment, with a kitchenette, a living area, and a large, comfortable bed. "Which is why I needed to tell Rock about my conversation with Oz afterwards."

"Did everything go well?" I ask distractedly. Thorn is pulling off his cut, which he tosses onto an arm of the couch.

"It did. Though there was some tension between me and Oz. It was touch and go for a bit."

"Why?" I frown. "I thought you weren't going to tell him I was there when you got Fowler?"

"I didn't." Thorn steps forward, pulling me into his arms. "But there's one thing I didn't tell you about my conversation with Oz."

"What's that?"

He reaches up and softly grazes my jaw with his thumb.

"I told him I'm in love with his daughter."

My eyes fill with tears. A lump forms in my throat I can hardly manage to speak around. "You did?" I whisper.

"Yeah." He chuckles. "I thought for a second he might send someone to murder me. But so far, so good."

"He'll have a hard time doing that," I say softly. "With me as your bodyguard."

"That he will," Thorn murmurs. "That he will."

"I was afraid this was the end," I whisper. A couple of tears fall, and Thorn brushes them from my cheeks. "I was almost wishing we could go back to the cabin."

"You aren't getting rid of me that easily, Sibéal." Thorn lifts me up, bracing me against the wall, and wraps my legs around his waist. "I haven't had a home since I left Ireland. Turns out, my home is you. At the cabin, or the safe house, or my place, or here. It doesn't matter."

From downstairs, a male voice shouts up at us. "Thorn!"

"Looks like you're being summoned," I say.

"Too bad." Thorn reaches over and cracks open the door. "Fuck off!" he calls. Closing the door again, he turns the lock. "We're not leaving this room until I get what I came for."

I giggle. "What's that?"

"I'm claiming my old lady," he growls, bending his face to mine. "Loudly, repeatedly, and until we're both too sore to move, the bed breaks, or the clubhouse burns down."

EPILOGUE

THORN

"I think my brain might literally be fried," Isabel groans, shutting her laptop.

"Last one, though, right?" I ask. "Now you have a month to recover before spring term."

"It might not be long enough," she sighs. "That was the hardest exam I've ever taken. God, I *hate* statistics."

"Good thing you're shut of it, then," I say, leaning down to kiss the top of her head. "Time to officially begin your Christmas break. Up you go. Let's get a move on."

"What are you talking about?" Isabel turns to look up at me, confusion on her face.

"I'm taking you on a Christmas holiday," I reply. "Bags are packed and in the car. Come on, let's go."

"Are you kidding?" She looks bewildered.

"Do I look like I'm kidding?" I shoot back, giving her a severe look. "Now, up with you. Don't make me lose my temper. I'm not a man who's used to being disobeyed."

I've been planning this trip for over a month. Somehow, I've managed to keep it a surprise from Isabel all this time. This is the end of her first term back at college, and successful completion of all her classes calls for a celebration. She's enrolled in an online associates degree program to become a nurse. She's still working on her prerequisites at the moment, but — with the exception of statistics — she seems to really like it so far. When she's not working on her online classes, she's racking up volunteer hours at the local hospital. She's worked incredibly hard this term, and I couldn't be more proud of her.

"Where are we going?" Isabel asks as I hustle her out to the garage and pile her into the car.

"It's a surprise."

"Seriously?" Isabel's mouth quirks up at me as I shut her door and go round to the other side.

"Yes, seriously. Now, settle in and stop asking questions. We'll be in the car for a bit."

THORN

* * *

It's about an hour's drive to where we're going, but I don't tell that to Isabel. In fact, I don't tell her anything else at all, despite the fact she's badgering me like crazy for the first twenty minutes. Eventually, she realizes I really am not going to divulge my secret, and begins to pout visibly until I laugh at her and tell her she's worse than a little kid.

It actually takes her much longer than it should to figure out our destination. But I can't say I fault her for that. After all, the last time she came here, she was blindfolded the entire way. I keep stealing glances over at her to see when the light bulb is going to come on. She finally puts two and two together when I slow down on a two-lane highway and turn into a driveway that's barely even visible from the road.

"Thorn!" she cries, her eyes shining. "Oh my gosh! We're going to the safe house!"

"We call it Connegut," I tell her. "Because of the river it's on. I thought we'd spend a week or so here. Go back to Tanner Springs a day or two after Christmas."

She lets out a little scream and bounces up and down in her seat a couple of times. "This is so perfect! I love this so much!"

This trip to Connegut is the last vacation we're likely to get together, before all hell breaks loose with the wedding in the spring. We're planning it for right after the end of Isabel's classes in May. Alix, Samantha, Sydney, Jenna, and Isabel's friend Deb have been doing most of the work, truth be told. My ma has been calling me weekly, to make sure Isabel hasn't come to her senses and called it all off. Ma's been putting off buying her ticket from Ireland until the last minute, even though Isabel has assured her repeatedly she's not going anywhere. Even Isabel's mother herself is making the trip back from Venezuela for the ceremony.

The Lords of Carnage will all be there, of course, as well as their old ladies and their families. And the Death Devils. Isabel jokes it'll be like a royal wedding. The joining of two houses, and all that shite.

As we pull up to the house in the late afternoon, it's just starting to get dark. All sorts of memories come flooding back to me, and looking over at Isabel I can tell they are for her, too. This is where it all started for us. Where I learned to hate her. And then, where I learned to love her.

We work as a team, carrying our bags and the groceries I packed into the house. The familiar musty smell greets us the second we walk in the door. I turn on the heat, and go out to haul in some firewood from the pile by the side of the house. When I come back in with an armload to start a fire, Isabel looks up from putting groceries away and smiles.

"You know, I used to watch you from the window while you were chopping wood," she grins.

"I went out there to get the hell away from you." I shake my head.

"God, you were an asshole when we first got here," Isabel laughs. She stands in the middle of the kitchen and twirls around, like a kid trying to get dizzy. "So cranky and brooding all the time."

"I was trying to keep my mind off how much I wanted to get into your pants," I point out. "Trying to keep my distance. Making you hate me was part of the strategy."

Her eyes twinkle. "After that first time we had sex, I started dressing skimpier, to try to tempt you into doing it again."

I come up and wrap my arms around her from behind. "You little vixen," I chastise her, and nip at her earlobe. "Well, it worked like a charm, so I hope you're happy."

"Very," she sighs. "You know, we should have started having sex way earlier," she continues dreamily. "Think of how many hours of boredom we could have saved ourselves. God, remember how bored we were? And you wouldn't even play cards with me or anything!"

"I don't remember refusing to play cards with you," I frown. "Why would I do that? Are you sure you aren't making things up?"

"Yes you did!" she insists. "Look, I distinctly remember finding cards in this drawer over here and asking you." Isabel crosses the room and goes to the end table next to the couch. Flopping down on the floor, she opens it.

"What're you doing?"

"Looking for a game to play!"

I'm perplexed. "You want to play a *game*? Are you joking? Don't you think we can find better ways to spend our time?"

But Isabel sees what she wants and lets out a shout of triumph.

"Candyland!" she crows gleefully, holding up a box and shaking at me.

"What're you playing at?" I frown. "What the hell is Candyland?"

"Are you kidding me? You mean you never played this?"

"I think I'd remember if I'd played something with a bollocks name like fuckin' Candyland!"

"It's a little kids game," she explains. "It's for like three year-olds. You don't need to know how to do anything except count to two, and know your colors." Isabel stands and sets the game on the coffee table. "We are totally playing this later."

"You *cannot* be asking me to play a game for three year-olds, Isabel," I protest, giving her my best cross look.

She cocks her head winks at me deviously. "How about *strip* Candyland, then?"

Isabel shoots me a dazzling grin, and just like that, I'm a goner.

"Fine," I sigh, mock-rolling my eyes. "We'll play your game."

Which we do. After dinner, Isabel sets out the board and the pieces and the little cards, and I'm playing fucking strip Candyland like it's a totally normal way to spend an evening. We have to make up the rules as we go along, of course, because the game is not exactly set up for this. At first, I'm regretting that I ever agreed to any of it. But then Isabel has to take off her shirt, and things start to get more interesting.

Somewhere around the middle of the game, Isabel points to something out the window. It's started to snow outside, in big, chicken-feather flakes. It's fucking beautiful. As we look at it together, I realize I'm happy as hell just being here with Isabel.

God, I used to *hate* this place. It almost makes me laugh now. But Isabel has changed that. Just like she's transformed almost every other aspect of my life. Now, I could almost stay here indefinitely, as long as she was here with me. Just the two of us, hidden away from the world.

Turns out, I'm better at strip Candyland than a man has any right to be. Eventually, Isabel is in her bra and panties, and I'm about to go fucking mad, sitting there and doing nothing about it. But she's insisting we have to finish the game, and having what is clearly a spectacular time winding me up.

"Ha!" she says during her turn. She holds out the card she's just picked up and shows me. Two red squares — that means I have to take something off. I'm still pretty much fully clothed except for boots, socks, and my cut, so it's time to remove my shirt. Which means it's time to show her my little surprise.

"So, I've got an early Christmas present for you," I tell her.

Isabel rolls her eyes. "You're just stalling for time."

"Not at all." I reach down to the hem of my shirt.

"Ooh, I'm liking this present already!" she grins. "But don't be dishonest. I won your shirt fair and square."

"Get your mind out of the gutter," I mock-bark at her. "And anyway, the shirt isn't the present. This is."

I pull off my shirt the rest of the way, revealing a bandage over my right pec. Isabel watches in confusion as I remove the tape to show her the tattoo I got done this morning at Rebel Ink, while she was studying for her last exam.

It's a starfish.

Isabel's eyes grow wide, her lips parting in surprised wonder.

"It seemed about time I got ink that represented you," I say. "I couldn't think of anything better than this. Your ma was right: you're the sea and the stars, Isabel. But you're also the creature that regenerates. You're resilient. You're unstoppable." I take her into my arms. "Best of all, you're mine."

Isabel's eyes are glowing in the light of the fire. "Yes, I am." She presses against me, her eyes growing hooded with desire. "I forfeit the game," she whispers to me. "Take me to bed, Mr. O'Malley."

* * *

"So, as it turns out, I sort of like Candyland," I say afterwards.

Isabel laughs, still breathing raggedly. "That's not exactly the way you're meant to play it. It's *significantly* more fun this way." She lays her head on my chest. "It's funny that there'd be a kids' game here, at an MC safe house."

I shrug. "Some of the Lords have kids. I imagine one of the families left it up here."

A moment of comfortable silence passes between us. We haven't talked about kids before, but I know they'll be coming sooner or later. There was a time when I would have said that was the last thing I'd ever want. But that was before I met Isabel. Before I had a home.

"I can picture you," she whispers. "Playing Candyland with a miniature version of you."

"Or of you," I point out.

"No. I want a boy first." I can hear the smile in her voice. "Named James. Jimmy."

My heart catches in my throat at the mention of my cousin. The cousin I couldn't protect. For the first time since it happened all those years ago, the thought of him doesn't send a slice of pain through me.

I'll always wish things had been different. That I could have seen Jimmy grow up. Become a man. Have a family of his own. Be a father. Maybe do a better job of it than most of the people around us managed to do.

If I'd been able to save Jimmy, I'd have never come to the States. Never joined the Lords. Never met Isabel.

"Jimmy, eh?" ask. The words come out hoarse. "Yeah, I could do that."

The time has come to stop regretting what could have been.

Living in the past will never bring Jimmy back. I can't bring him back.

But maybe in some small way, naming his future cousin after him will.

Together, Isabel and I can do our best to make his memory live on.

BOOKS BY DAPHNE LOVELING

Motorcycle Club Romance

Los Perdidos MC
Fugitives MC
Throttle: A Stepbrother Romance
Rush: A Stone Kings Motorcycle Club Romance
Crash: A Stone Kings Motorcycle Club Romance
Ride: A Stone Kings Motorcycle Club Romance
Stand: A Stone Kings Motorcycle Club Romance
STONE KINGS MOTORCYCLE CLUB: The Complete Collection

GHOST: Lords of Carnage MC
HAWK: Lords of Carnage MC
BRICK: Lords of Carnage MC
GUNNER: Lords of Carnage MC

Sports Romance

Getting the Down
Snap Count
Zone Blitz

Paranormal Romance

Untamed Moon

Collections

Daphne's Delights: The Paranormal Collection
Daphne's Delights: The Billionaire Collection

ABOUT THE AUTHOR

Daphne Loveling is a small-town girl who moved to the big city as a young adult in search of adventure. She lives in the American Midwest with her fabulous husband and the two cats who own them.

Someday, she hopes to retire to a sandy beach and continue writing with sand between her toes.

Printed in Great Britain
by Amazon